His gaze skipped over the two nurses he knew and landed on the third one, who sat a little to the side of the other two. Her head was down as she looked at something on one of the computers.

Lyndsey?

He blinked, his steps slowing. Lyndsey was working here? Why had she not said something when he'd seen her on Friday?

A thread of anger went through him, and he stalked over to the desk. Faith greeted him immediately. "Hey, have you met our newest team member?"

Team? He'd thought he and Lyndsey were a team at one time. Had thought they'd be able to stay in touch and maybe even reconnect in the future, but she'd cut off any chance of that happening. He wasn't sure what she was playing at, but there was no way her working here could be a coincidence.

"Actually, Ms. McKinna and I went to high school together."

She was now looking at him, the guilt in her eyes telling him all he needed to know.

He addressed her, unable to force a smile to his lips. "Can I talk to you for a minute?"

Dear Reader,

As a mom, I know I would do almost anything to protect my children. But what if one of them has a health issue that needs to be addressed? What if getting them the help they need means reconnecting with an ex that you haven't seen in fifteen years but haven't quite gotten over?

That is the position that Lyndsey finds herself in. Her fifteen-year-old son has a rare condition that is slowly damaging his hearing. Without surgery, he will almost certainly lose it all together. When Misha, an ENT specialist, shows up at her hospital, she is forced to make a hard decision, but this time she has no intention of falling for the surgeon again.

Thank you so much for joining Misha and Lyndsey as they address issues from their past and figure out how to work together, both at the hospital and to save her son's hearing. And maybe, just maybe, they'll each find a way to heal from the hurts of the past and discover a spark of something special. I hope you love reading their story as much as I loved writing it!

Happy reading!

Love,

Tina Beckett

THE SURGEON SHE
COULD NEVER FORGET

TINA BECKETT

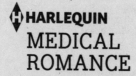

HARLEQUIN
MEDICAL
ROMANCE

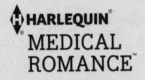

HARLEQUIN®
MEDICAL ROMANCE™

Recycling programs
for this product may
not exist in your area.

ISBN-13: 978-1-335-59488-4

The Surgeon She Could Never Forget

Harlequin Enterprises ULC
22 Adelaide St. West, 41st Floor
Toronto, Ontario M5H 4E3, Canada
www.Harlequin.com

Printed in U.S.A.

Three-time Golden Heart® Award finalist **Tina Beckett** learned to pack her suitcases almost before she learned to read. Born to a military family, she has lived in the United States, Puerto Rico, Portugal and Brazil. In addition to traveling, Tina loves to cuddle with her pug, Alex, spend time with her family and hit the trails on her horse. Learn more about Tina from her website or friend her on Facebook.

Books by Tina Beckett

Harlequin Medical Romance

California Nurses

The Nurse's One-Night Baby

New York Bachelor's Club

Consequences of Their New York Night
The Trouble with the Tempting Doc

Starting Over with the Single Dad
Their Reunion to Remember
One Night with the Sicilian Surgeon
From Wedding Guest to Bride?
A Family Made in Paradise
The Vet, the Pup and the Paramedic

Visit the Author Profile page
at Harlequin.com for more titles.

For moms everywhere

PROLOGUE

"WHY DO YOU have to go?" If Lyndsey Marshall asked the question enough times, surely that resolute finality she saw written on Misha's face would change, and he'd go back to the warm, funny guy she loved so very much. He had to realize how much he stood to lose—how much *they* stood to lose—by his moving back to Belarus with his family. They'd just graduated from high school a week ago, had made plans for the future. One in which she'd envisioned the two of them being together forever. Having children. A home. "Surely you could get a student visa for college. Can't you stay on your own? I'm sure your parents would understand. And my mom could let you stay with—"

"I must. My parents must get their visa

situation straightened out or they could be deported and denied reentry later on. And my dad…" His throat moved as if some powerful emotion swept through him. "Maybe someday…"

His words drifted away, but all she heard was her own father's voice five years ago telling her that he had to leave, but that they would have all kinds of fun together. But they never had. Instead, he'd started another family with another woman he'd met on one of his business trips. His calls to his daughter had been few and far between and filled with, "Hey, someday we need to…" Only those "somedays" had never materialized. His new daughter deserved his love and attention, but Lyndsey evidently didn't.

She was never going to accept that answer again. Not from Misha. She couldn't. Not if she was to survive his leaving.

"No. Not someday. If you leave now, it's over between us."

If anything, the withdrawal she'd sensed in him grew. She knew she should stop talking, but it was as if all the impotent rage she'd felt when her dad left came boiling out, pushing words she'd never be able to retract past the ball in her throat. She knew she wasn't being fair, but the hurt in her was so big. So overwhelming.

God, if he left her too…

But he's going to. You know he is.

He reached out to touch her, but she batted his hand away trying not to break down like she'd done five years ago when her father broke the news to her. If he touched her, she'd be lost. She'd fall apart, just like she had back then.

This time she wasn't going to be staring at her cell phone for days and months on end willing it to ring. Willing him to come back. If he was going to leave, she wanted it to be a clean cut that might at least have a chance to heal.

"Please, Misha…" She drew a deep breath. "Leave if it's what you have to do. But don't prolong it. Don't call me. Don't contact me. Just…" her arms waved in the air like an injured sparrow. "…don't." The word ended on a sob before she could press her hand to her mouth to contain the sound.

She leaped out of the car and ran up her

front driveway, never looking back. Pushed through the front door, slamming it behind her as she bolted up the stairs to her room, vaguely hearing her mother calling to her. But she didn't stop. She kept running, mentally, long after she'd thrown herself onto the bed, sobbing in earnest until no more tears came, only dry racking cries that hurt her chest and stole the breath from her lungs. Then she lay there, ignoring her mom's soft knock, her mind and emotions completely numb.

After what seemed like an hour, she finally pried herself from the mattress and went to the window, hoping beyond hope that his car would still be there. That he would have changed his mind. After all, his dad was a doctor here in Lafayette. Surely he wouldn't leave his practice behind and drag his family halfway across the world?

According to Misha, that's exactly what he was prepared to do.

When she peered through the sheer curtains, the spot where he'd been parked was empty. As empty as her heart now was.

She didn't know how she'd get through

it, but she'd show him that she was a survivor. She'd survived her father leaving. She'd survive this too.

Only it didn't matter. Because Misha wouldn't actually be there to see her rise and conquer. Somehow that just made it worse.

When the light tapping on her door returned, it made her flinch, and she ground her palms into her swollen eyes to hopefully erase any sign of her tears. Except when she opened the door, her mother was there, seeing right past her smile and pulling her into the safe haven of her arms. Lyndsey promptly fell apart all over again.

But this was the last time. The last time she would shed tears for Mikhail Lukyanov. Because tomorrow she was going to get up and start gluing her shattered world back together again. One tiny fragment at a time.

CHAPTER ONE

CHERT VOZMI!

MIKHAIL LUKYANOV DROPPED into his office chair, muttering about how far off the rails his day had already gone. And he'd only just arrived for his very first day after opening his own practice. It was funny how Louisiana had always been home, despite the fact that after high school he'd spent five years in Belarus. In the midst of finding out his dad had leukemia, it turned out that his dad's work visa to the States—unbeknownst to any of them—had been forged by a family friend who claimed he had an "in" with the US consulate.

No one had caught the problem until Misha's dad went to renew their visas and a quick check came back saying there was

no record of a work visa for Dmitry Lukyanov. They had no choice but to return to
Belarus. Fortunately, Dmitry was eventually able to prove that he'd immigrated to
the States in good faith and had been offered a chance to return. Except that by
then, five years had gone by, and after a
long, hard fight, his dad's leukemia had
become a monster that could no longer be
controlled with chemo, and he'd been too
ill to travel. When his dad passed away a
few months later, Misha decided to make
his own trek to the States, with his mom's
blessing, and finish medical school there.
Which he'd finally finished three years
ago. Then he'd opted to spend another two
years studying surgical options for hearing
loss under one of the top surgeons in the
United States.

And here he was back in southern Louisiana. Lafayette was about fifty miles from
where he'd graduated high school, but he
hadn't been able to bear moving back there
with all the memories. He'd toyed several
times with the idea of visiting and trying
to find Lyndsey, but as the years went by,

he finally decided it was better to leave things alone. Why barge in and disrupt her life again after all this time? Plus, the idea of seeing her happily married with a passel of children made his gut churn.

He shook off the thoughts as one of his office staff poked her head in. "We were able to juggle your schedule, Doctor. Most of the patients you missed this morning are able to come back this afternoon. All except one, who said she'd wait for as long as it took for you to get here. And we canceled your surgery for this morning at the hospital."

A swear word flashed through his mind. He hated that someone had been waiting on him for over three hours, especially on his first day. But it had taken almost two-and-a-half hours to get the loaner car when his own vehicle had refused to start that morning.

Maybe this was some deity's idea of a joke, forcing a now rigidly inflexible Misha to loosen his grip on his sense of order. But it was what had gotten him through those first horrible months back in Belarus, when his grief over his dad's diagnosis and how he and Lyndsey had left things had almost overwhelmed him. Somehow he'd gotten through it. And now whatever he and Lyndsey had once had was firmly in the past.

"Is she in a waiting room?"

"Yes. The son will be the patient, though."

"Name?"

"Brody McKinna."

He stood. "Okay, which room?"

"Exam room three."

He mentally went through the layout of the set of rooms that comprised his practice. "When you get a chance, could you print a list of my patients, so I have an idea of who's coming when?"

Nelly smiled and handed him a sheet of paper on a clipboard. "Already done." She gave him a smile. "And don't worry about it. Things tend to work out the way they're supposed to."

Misha used to believe that, but he didn't any longer. But he also didn't have time to stand here and argue with someone who was just trying to make him feel better. So he smiled and thanked her before heading down the hallway toward his first patient of the day.

She was nervous. So terribly nervous.

She'd never expected to see Misha again, much less find out he was the hospital's new ENT and had specialized training in hearing loss cases. But it wasn't for her. When her son's doctor had heard about a new doctor who was coming to Lafayette with great credentials, he'd written down the man's name. She'd stared at the slip of paper in shock, unable to breathe for a second or two. Then her fingertip had slowly traced over the letters on the paper. Surely not. It had to be a fluke. But what were the chances of another Misha Lukyanov coming to Louisiana.

And now he was here. At the very hospital where she'd worked for the last year. An hour from where she'd grown up. Where they'd graduated from high school.

It would be pretty hard to avoid each other when they were going to be working on the same floor.

If he declined to take on her son as his patient today, would seeing her day in and day out make him change his mind? She could go to another doctor if she had to, but the waits were long. And with Misha being new to the hospital, surely he would be more likely to have openings in his schedule, right? And Brody's condition had progressed far faster than expected. Thankfully his doctor had been able to wrangle an appointment with Misha today.

But she'd come alone, while Brody was in school. She didn't want him to be witness to whatever reaction her high school sweetheart might have to seeing her again. She'd been pretty harsh the last time she'd seen him. And pretty broken up inside after he'd left.

She'd paid the price for the rabbit hole she'd gone down after he left the country.

She squirmed in her chair as she waited for someone to update her on how much longer they thought it would be until he arrived. She'd been the only one who'd opted to wait. And she would wait here a week, if she had to.

You can do this. You have *to do this.*

She couldn't let Brody suffer because of her pride. Her son was an innocent party to all that had transpired since his birth. And if Misha hadn't left, Brody would never have been born. So no. She wouldn't go back and undo the past. Even with all that had happened leading up to his birth.

The door to the exam room opened so suddenly that she flinched, something she didn't do as often as she used to, and she gritted her teeth over the muscle memory that still provoked the response.

And then he was there in the doorway, as large as life. He'd put on a bit of weight since the last time she saw him. But it looked good on him. The tall, lanky boy she'd known in high school had morphed into a man. One that was devastatingly attractive and whose unwavering eyes found hers with the precision of a scalpel. She forced herself to hold still, afraid to even breathe, even as a boatload of emotions resurfaced with a vengeance. She bit her lip as her eyes skimmed his shoulders, unable to stop them from venturing lower…

"Lyndsey?"

His deep voice made her gaze jerk back to his as the low tones rolled over her name in that strange but wonderful accent that used to turn her inside out. He would murmur it as his lips slowly trailed across her cheek. As he chuckled at something she said. As he said goodbye that last day. Another wave of emotion—stronger this time—rose, and she fought against it. Even as she noted the empty ring finger on his left hand, she knew there was no going back. For either of them. She needed to remember that. She was not here for herself. She was here for Brody.

It had become a litany she'd repeated for the last week and a half as she'd waited for the new doctor's arrival in Lafayette.

She forced herself to nod. "Yes."

His jaw tightened, glancing down at a piece of paper in his hand. "I'm not sure what this is, but I have a lot of patients to see, and I don't have time for..."

She filled in the word he hadn't said: *You. I don't have time for* you.

Neither had her father. Another pang

hit her. Her half sister and brother were virtual strangers to her. She'd only seen them a handful of times in all these years. And with her father's passing last year, she didn't see that changing anytime soon.

"It's not for me. It's for my son."

"And where is he?" He glanced again at the paper. "Brody… McKinna?"

She licked her lips, hoping he didn't recognize the last name. "I—I didn't bring him. If you threw me out of your office, I didn't want him to be here. I know you're busy, but please just hear me out. I brought his chart." She offered him the manila envelope in her hand.

Misha stared at her for a long moment before he took it and lowered himself onto the rolling stool that put him at eye level with her.

Eye level was good, right? Except when those eyes were electric blue and evidently still capable of sending shivers of heat through her.

At least he hadn't thrown her out. Hadn't told her to take Brody's chart and find some other specialist. Not yet, anyway.

He spread the paperwork on the exam table next to him before putting on some reading glasses. If anything, those dark frames made him look even more devastatingly handsome. Her insides shifted at the effect he still had on her. She felt shaky and out of sorts with him being so close, his knee almost touching hers. But she needed to get control of herself. This Misha was not the carefree kid he'd been in school. The one with a smile that just wouldn't quit and a sense of humor that used to keep her in stitches.

No, this man had a deep furrow between his brows that was there as he studied Brody's chart. And he'd not smiled. Not even one time. In fact, it was as if he was totally unaffected by her presence.

Would she rather him try to worm his way back into her affections?

No. Not after all this time. After all that had happened since he'd left.

His finger tapped one of the sheets. "Otosclerosis?"

"Yes. Progressing much faster than anticipated. We thought we'd have at least a year to get things in place to save his hearing, but it looks like he may not have that much time. He's only fifteen and I can't imagine—"

His head came up. "Your son is fifteen?"

She swallowed. Oh, God, she'd hoped to avoid this particular discussion.

"Y-yes. His birthday is in March."

His face was still as he mentally did the math. When his eyes speared hers again, the blue irises had chilled and there was ring of anger in them. "Despite the timeline, I take it he's not mine. Where's his father?"

The question wasn't exactly something a doctor should ask, but she understood.

Before she could answer, though, he spoke again as if he'd just realized something. "McKinna.... Is it *Wade* McKinna? The guy who asked you to prom right before we started dating?"

Leave it to Misha to put two and two together so quickly. Wade had been high school quarterback and she'd been flattered when he'd asked her to the dance. But even then, she'd only had eyes for

Misha. But once he left for Belarus, Wade had stepped in with a show of empathy and offered the comfort she'd so desperately needed. She'd been sobbing, clinging to his shoulders. When he kissed her, she didn't resist, but she needed something that no one could give her. One thing led to another as she tried to bury her grief and she wound up pregnant. Wade immediately offered marriage, said he loved her and would love their child.

And Misha, in her eyes, was gone forever. So she'd said yes, praying she'd somehow learn to feel something for Wade.

Only it wasn't love she came to feel. Because her idea of love and his were poles apart.

When she realized Misha was still looking at her, she forced herself to answer. "Yes. But he's no longer in the picture. He won't be making any decisions about Brody's care."

"I see."

His face was hard as he turned his attention back to the pages in front of him.

"What exactly is it you're expecting me to do for Brody?"

Was he serious? There was no way he didn't know. "I'm hoping you'll take him on as a patient. Perform his surgery."

His eyes closed for a second before re-opening. "There are other surgeons who could do it. Why me?"

She understood why he was asking, but she needed him to know that it had nothing to do with their past. "Because his other ENT says you have a good reputation and trained under the best of the best in this particular surgery. And I don't want to up-root Brody from his friends and school. He's dealt with enough in his life with his…" Realizing she was saying more than she'd meant to, she ended with, "…getting his diagnosis, I mean." The less she talked about Wade the better. She didn't want to dredge up that painful past any more than she wanted to revisit the last time she set eyes on Misha.

They were both over and done, and she couldn't change either outcome.

Except her body's crazy reaction to him was putting her on shaky ground when it came to being around him. Surely, it was just the shock of seeing him again. Those emotions would slink back to whatever dark corner they'd emerged from, right? Especially since there was no sign of any renewed attraction from his end.

"I need time to look over his chart, and I'd like to consult further with his other ENT." A muscle worked in his cheek. "And I'll need to meet Brody."

The way he said it made her think it was the last thing he wanted to do. But she didn't care.

Hope and desperation made her reach out and grab his hand before realizing what she was doing. She let go of it just as quickly, before saying in a low voice. "Misha, please don't hold our past and what happened afterward against my son. He played no part in my decisions."

A muscle ticked in his jaw as he leveled his gaze at her. "I would never blame a child for things over which he had no control. Over who his mother chose to be with."

She knew how it had to look to him. That she had fallen into bed with someone almost on the heels of his departure. But things weren't always like they seemed. And he could be mad at her as much as he wanted, as long as it didn't affect Brody.

He sighed and stood up. "As it is, I'm already late for many appointments today, so if there's nothing else…"

And just like that, he'd dismissed her. As if it was the easiest thing to do.

If only she could be more like that. But this time she needed to push for what she needed. Because her son's hearing was at stake.

"So you'll at least consider taking him on?"

"Like I said, I'll need to take my schedule into consideration, since I'm still getting the feel of things at the hospital. But stop at the front desk and make another appointment. This time, bring your son with you."

She stood as well. "I will."

"I'll see you soon."

As he went through the door, she almost gave a sharp laugh. Yes, he would. And he didn't know how soon. She hadn't mentioned that she worked at the hospital as well. She'd meant to throw out some humorous quip about them now being colleagues, but his attitude had not invited humor, or anything else. So he was just going to have to learn about it on Monday morning.

And she had no idea if working in his department would help Brody's cause or blow her chances completely out of the water.

Misha's Monday morning was already going much better than his Friday had. He glanced at the nurse's desk on his way through Louisiana Southern's busy ENT department. He'd definitely been thrown into the deep end. He already had two surgeries scheduled for today. A tympanomastoidectomy to treat a stubborn ear infection and a cochlear implant. The implant surgery would take a couple of hours in and of itself.

And he was still trying to learn names and faces of the people he was working with.

As his gaze skipped over the two nurses he recognized, they landed on the third one, who sat a little to the right of the other two. Her head was down as she looked at something on her computer, and a long wavy strand of hair rested against the side of her face, having escaped its confinement. He recognized that hair. And the graceful way her neck curved as she tilted her head to read something on the screen in front of her.

Lyndsey?

He blinked, his steps slowing. Lyndsey was working *here*? Why had she not said something when he'd seen her on Friday?

A thread of anger went through him, and he stalked over to the desk. Faith smiled at him and then reached to tap Lyndsey on the shoulder. "Hey, Lynds, have you met our newest team member?"

Team? As in they would be working in the same department? He wasn't sure what she was playing at, but there was no way her working here could be a coincidence. Or she would have mentioned it on Friday. So why hadn't she?

"Actually, Ms. McKinna and I went to high school together. And I had no idea she was working here."

She was now looking at him, the guilt in her eyes telling him all he needed to know. He addressed her, unable to force a smile to his lips. "Actually, can I talk to you for a minute?"

Faith looked surprised, while Meredith, the other nurse, lifted her brows. He'd been short and he knew it, probably not making the best impression on the pair, but he didn't have time to dance around and try to figure out what was going on. He wanted to hear it. From Lyndsey.

"Of course." She sent the two nurses an apologetic glance and came out from behind the desk, her hands tugging the hem of her scrubs over her backside. If anything, it just emphasized curves that still had the power to make his mouth go dry. *Dammit!*

He strode ahead of her to avoid staring

at it, shoving his hands into the pockets of his jeans, before rounding the corner and stopping out of view of the desk.

"What is going on here? You said nothing about working at Louisiana Southern during your appointment on Friday."

She moistened her lips, and he did his damnedest not to fixate on the move. Instead, he propped his shoulder against the wall to his right and waited.

"You didn't ask me."

He stared at her. "Try again."

"Okay, look, I know. I should have mentioned it. But you weren't actually very approachable during our appointment."

"Finding out you slept with the high school quarterback almost immediately after I left the country was...well, not what I would have expected from you."

Her chin jerked up. "Not that my actions were of any concern of yours once you broke things off between us—"

"I seem to remember it being you who asked me never to contact you again."

Although he could understand why she had. He'd been in shock over the spiraling events that had sent his world on a collision course.

She paused for a minute as if pulling herself together. "What's done is done, Misha. Neither one of us can change the past. Can't we just go on from here?"

"As in…?"

Her face turned pink. "As in working together as colleagues?"

That brought him back to why he'd wanted to talk to her. "So you're going to tell me this is all one big coincidence?"

"Actually it is. I've been working here for a year. So unless you were angling for this job as a way of getting back in contact with me…"

Which is what he'd just basically accused her of doing. "No. But I did want to come back to Louisiana. New York was too big of a city for me."

And the fact that he'd broken off a brief relationship with a nurse at that hospital had made the offer at Louisiana Southern look even more attractive. But he didn't want to go into any of that. Especially not with Lyndsey.

"I get it. And I'll be honest. Brody needs this surgery, and I'm willing to do almost anything it takes to make sure it happens."

One of his brows lifted before he could stop it. She hadn't meant that the way it had sounded, despite all kinds of X-rated images that were now dancing around in his skull.

Her face suddenly suffused with color as if she'd been privy to his thoughts. "That didn't come out quite right. I—I mean finding him the help he needs. My pride means nothing compared to what awaits him without this surgery. And if that means asking someone who hates me to take him on—"

"I don't hate you, Lyndsey." His heart contracted even as he said the words. Because it was true. No matter how that shard of jealousy over her and Wade McKinna had dug deep into his flesh, he wasn't going to punish her son for it. "I told you I would never turn down a patient, especially a child, out of spite." He studied her. "You didn't know me as well as I thought you did, evidently."

"I thought I did. But…" She shrugged.

"People aren't always who you think they are. And Wade, well…"

Something about the way she talked about the man gave him pause. Even after all his years in the States, there were still nuances of the language he didn't always grasp. And he didn't have time to work through it right now. She'd said Brody's dad was no longer in the picture, so she and Wade must have split up. But how long ago?

Did it matter?

Hell, he didn't know how he felt about having to see her every time he was at the hospital. She'd hurt him badly fifteen years ago. Had written him off without even hearing him out. But then he knew he'd hurt her too. But it couldn't have been helped at the time. He could have told her about his dad, but somehow even voicing the word *leukemia* had been beyond him at that moment.

He sighed. "I don't have time to hash all of this out with you right now, but we do need to talk if we're going to work together on a daily basis. Do you have plans tonight?"

"Tonight?"

Damn, he hadn't phrased that well. "I'm not talking about a date. I just don't want there to be any misunderstandings about what is happening here." He tightened his jaw. "If I do the surgery, it will change nothing between us on a personal level."

She licked her lips. "I wouldn't expect it to. Nor would I want it to any more than you would."

He hoped to hell that was true. Because her scent was wrapping around him in a way that spelled danger. The sooner he left the vicinity, the better. "Good. So tonight? You have plans?"

"No. Brody has a club meeting after school, so maybe we can meet at the coffee shop next door. Say at five? It's when I get off work."

"Five it is. I'll see you then."

"Yes. See you."

They stood there for a few seconds as if unsure who was going to walk away from whom. Then Lyndsey spun around and headed back the way she'd come, leaving him to continue down the corridor on his way to his first patient's room. All he could think was that the day that had started out with such promise had just imploded in spectacular fashion.

His cochlear surgery had taken longer than expected, and when he glanced at his watch, he saw he was already five minutes late for his meeting with Lyndsey and he didn't have her cell phone number. He discarded his surgical scrubs and made his way through the hospital exit, before turning right toward the coffee shop. He was now ten minutes late. As someone who was particular about appointment times, spacing his further apart than most doctors so that he wouldn't fall behind, he hated being tardy. Of course, Friday hadn't worked out well in that regard either.

When he arrived, the scent of strong coffee hit his nose with a welcome sense of familiarity, and he spotted Lyndsey already hunched over a cup of brew. He gave her a nod of acknowledgment before putting his order in and then heading over to her table. "Sorry I'm late. Surgery ran longer than I expected."

"I know." She gave a quick smile. "I work there too, remember?"

Of course. She would have known that it ran over. He wasn't sure how he felt about her knowing things about his life and routine. But there was no changing it now. She was still in her scrubs, but any hope that they might dull the attraction that hummed just below the surface was quickly crushed. Because he'd once known every inch of that body. Becoming a mother had only enhanced those dips and curves. He steeled his voice to respond in as normal a tone as he could muster.

"Yes, I remember." The barista came over with his coffee and set it in front of him. He gave her a quick thank-you before turning his attention back to the woman in front of him. Studying her for a moment, he noticed fine lines next to her eyes that spoke of either worry or concentration. Her hair was still long and wavy, like it had been in school, the strands catching the light and turning them honey gold. She'd freed them from the confines of the clip she'd had on earlier. And hell if he didn't remember all too well threading those locks between his fingers when he kissed her. His fingers curled into his palms as he tried to banish the sharp sense of need that flooded him over the memory.

She took a drink of her coffee before saying, "I'm sorry. I'm sure seeing me at the nurses' desk today was a shock. But I promise I'm not stalking you, despite how much I want Brody to have this surgery."

That thought had never even crossed his mind. He leaned forward. "Lyndsey, even if he isn't a candidate for surgery, there are other options."

"If you're talking about an implant, I know that. But he's experienced natural hearing, and I think it would be harder for him to adjust to the change in perception. Plus, from what I read, there's a chance for ossification of the cochlea, after implant surgery, right? And the electrical current can affect facial nerves?"

He was impressed. "You've done quite a bit of research."

"I've read everything I can get my hands on. If he can have surgery before his hearing loss is profound, it provides the best option to preserve what hearing he has left."

"You are correct." This was not someone who just took a medical professional's words as coming from God. This was someone who was willing to stretch her knowledge and make the best decisions based on research rather than emotion.

"So...?"

"I still have to look through everything. I need to make an informed decision too. The last thing I want to do is go in there and do something that does more harm to your son than good.

"His name is Brody."

Yes, Brody McKinna. He knew the boy's name. It was already burned into his subconscious with a fire that scorched its way from his chest to his gut. She'd had a child that should have been theirs, had the fates been kinder to them. But they hadn't. And the fact that she'd jumped from his arms right into someone like Wade's just about killed him. He hadn't liked the star football player from the moment she'd mentioned that he had asked her to the prom. Yes, she'd said no, but on some level she must have been attracted to the guy, right?

Even when she'd been involved with him?

He would never know the answer to that, because he was never going to ask the question. Best to just put it behind him.

"Okay... Brody...would benefit more from a measured approach rather than a rush to surgery. Which is why I need some time."

She blinked at him, her blue eyes filling with a moisture that punched buttons he thought he'd deleted not moments earlier.

"So you were serious about taking him on?"

"There was never any question. Like I said on Friday, I would never penalize someone for things over which they had no control."

He hadn't meant the words as a jab at their past, but if it came across that way, so be it. He'd had no control over whether he stayed or went. He'd had to help his family during a time of crisis. In his mind, there'd been no other option. And as his dad fought his illness and his mom leaned on him more and more for comfort and decision making, he knew that decision had been the right one.

So, what to do about Lyndsey and Brody? He sure as hell wasn't going to tell her to leave and never contact him again, that was for sure.

He was going to "do unto others as he wished she'd done unto him." Wasn't that basically what that old sage piece of advice meant? Yes, it was. And he was going to do his best to follow it, even if it was the second hardest thing he'd done in his life.

CHAPTER TWO

LYNDSEY PARKED IN the lot outside of the emergency department of the hospital. It provided the most direct route to where she worked. As she entered the space, she caught sight of a team rushing a young girl toward the double doors she'd just come through. The bulge of her abdomen as they went by said she was expecting a child. Just then, she caught the unmistakable gurgled wheeze of someone who was struggling to breathe and failing. Again and again it came, and a clench of fear gripped her, as she stared at the passing gurney.

She recognized that sound. Had *lived* that sound while pregnant with Brody.

A touch to her arm made her recoil until she caught herself. Misha was looking down at her with a strange look in his eyes. "Come. I need you."

A second later he was striding after the gurney. She swallowed when she realized he meant he needed her help with the patient. She hurried to catch up with him just as he reached the nearest curtained-off area. The closer she got, the more pronounced the stridor became.

Restricted airway. A true medical emergency.

"We couldn't intubate," one of the EMTs said. "The swelling is too much."

"What happened?" Misha's voice was calm and measured, no sign of panic or hurry. Unlike Lyndsey's own chaotic thoughts.

"Car accident. No seatbelt, and it looks like she hit the dashboard."

She moved closer, waiting for him to tell her what to do, even as her fear grew in time with the girl's struggle to draw every breath. With every second the baby in her belly went without precious oxygen.

Misha was already examining the girl. She was about the age Lyndsey was when she'd been pregnant with Brody. God. It was a wonder he'd survived. It was a wonder he hadn't been left with some kind of deficit afterward.

She put her hand to her throat as if the young woman's struggle was her own all over again.

"We need to help the baby." Her voice came out thin and thready.

He shot her a glance. "And we will. I need a trach kit." He frowned. "Now!"

Lyndsey quickly forced her hand away from her neck and donned gloves. Regathering her composure, she found the kit.

She ripped it open and sloshed the antiseptic solution over the girl's neck, the purple bruising and swelling telling a story that made her swallow. They needed to get this done before the swelling closed off the area completely.

She handed Misha a scalpel and watched as he felt for the correct spot and then with unerring accuracy made the cut through skin and cartilage, as she waited with the tubing components.

He held his hand out, and she gave them to him.

It took him two tries, and he muttered something she recognized as Russian before the tubing slid home.

She hadn't realized how tense she still was until the girl drew her first unencumbered breath. Then Lyndsey released her own in a rush, her limbs feeling suddenly trembly and weak.

A nurse stuck her head in. "Obstetrics is on their way."

"Good." Misha gave her another glance, his frown deepening.

God. She didn't want him to see her fall apart. She hadn't felt this way in a long time. Had thought that the years of therapy after her disastrous marriage had banished most of her reactions to unexpected situations.

It had to be this girl's pregnancy bringing back the trauma of what had happened during her own pregnancy?

She wasn't sure. She just knew that for a second she hadn't been able to breathe, and the old panic had risen up, swamping her. Or maybe Misha's presence back in her life had somehow unearthed the memories. But why? He'd never treated her badly. And he'd definitely never hurt her physically.

"Are you okay?" he asked.

"Yes. I'm just late for my shift, and I…" What else could she say? She didn't want to tell him what had happened to her. Couldn't bear the look of pity that would surely come her way. She'd encountered plenty of those looks as she'd recounted her story from the witness stand of a courtroom.

His eyes narrowed, and she did her best to hold herself still and force a smile that was as fake as her words. But he simply nodded. "Go. I've got this. I'll need to get her to surgery to finish up anyway once obstetrics checks the baby's vitals."

"Thank you."

Through a mist of nausea, she somehow made her legs carry her from the room and made it to the nearest bathroom. She raced into a stall and vomited into the toilet, the feeling of relief immediate as if the act worked to release her emotions.

Afterward, she washed her face and rinsed out her mouth, and found a breath mint in her purse. Looking at herself, she realized she was as pale as death. Hopefully, it wasn't visible to anyone but her.

She waited a moment or two longer, then, still shaky, but at least rid of the crippling fear and sense of foreboding, she exited the bathroom. Somehow, she made her way to her department and got through the first part of her shift until her lunch break. There was no sign of Misha, and she was glad. He'd almost witnessed something that would have mortified her.

She got a light lunch from the cafeteria and took it out into the courtyard, finding a spot to sit away from others. She lowered herself onto the concrete bench and thought about the events of the morning. She hadn't reacted like that in a long, long time. Maybe Misha's presence really had triggered something, but why?

As if she'd summoned him, he was suddenly there. "Care if I join you for a minute?"

Rather than try to speak, she shrugged,

horrified that the shaky feeling from the ER was returning. But at least she wasn't nauseous this time around.

He studied her. "What happened?"

Her heart clenched for a second before she realized he wasn't talking about her past with Wade. Rather, he was referring to the emergency trach procedure.

She sidestepped the question. "Is she okay? The baby?"

"Yes, they both are. But are you?"

Lyndsey swallowed. "Of course. Why do you ask?"

"You know why."

Damn. He'd always been able to read her. The fact that he still could irked her in a way she couldn't quite understand.

"It's always distressing to see someone on the knife's edge of life and death."

"Yes. But surely you've seen that many times before."

She had. She wouldn't be able to work as a nurse if she couldn't handle terrible outcomes—those times when nothing they did succeeded in saving a patient's life.

"Yes. But that doesn't mean I'm hardened to it." For some reason, she didn't want him to know what a colossal mistake she'd made by becoming involved with Wade. Part of it was she didn't want to relive it again by telling him. But there was also part of her that didn't want him to know how long she'd waited before leaving the relationship.

He didn't say anything for a long minute. "I think maybe it's more than that. But I won't press you for something you don't want to give."

He never had. It was one of the biggest differences between Misha and Wade. And she wondered all over again how she could have fallen for her ex-husband's words. Maybe she'd been trying to get back at Misha for leaving her. If so, she'd only ended up hurting herself. And Brody.

She decided to at least answer this question truthfully. "Thank you. I appreciate that."

He drew a deep breath and then looked at her. "So. Tell me more about Brody."

Glad to talk about something other than herself, she talked about his condition, filling him in on how he'd been diagnosed. Otosclerosis was rare. Very rare. And it tended to be inherited. If one parent had the gene, there was a chance of passing it down to their offspring. Lyndsey had gone through genetic testing, in case she decided to have more children, but her test had come back clear. And there was no way she was going to ask Wade to take a test. She did not want him in Brody's life in any way, shape or form.

"It started in his right ear. Originally, they thought it was the remnants of an ear infection. But then his left ear started to show signs of slight hearing loss as well. That's where we are now. He's had a tympanogram to measure hearing conduction to his eardrum and a CT scan, both of which seem to confirm otosclerosis."

"Yes, that follows the pattern. He's on the younger end of the spectrum." Misha said, as if thinking out loud. He glanced at her again. "You already know surgery involves putting in a prosthesis to bypass the stapes, then."

The stapes was one of the three bones

of the middle ear. And in otosclerosis, that bone gradually becomes cemented or "stuck" in place and unable to transmit sound vibrations.

"Yes." Before he had a chance to say anything, she continued. "I also know there's a chance that surgery could make his hearing worse. Which is why I'd rather have it done in his right ear first, before attempting the other ear."

"I would totally agree with that plan." He sat back. "Now. Tell me about Brody."

Her head tilted. "But I just—"

"No. Not about his condition. I want to know about him as a person."

"But why?"

He smiled. "You chided me for referring to him as your son and made sure I knew his name. So I want to know more about him." He touched her hand. "Believe it or not, I do view my patients as people."

His fingers were warm on her skin, and it was hard not to turn her hand palm-side up and link her fingers through his. But the days of doing that had long passed. And Lyndsey couldn't afford to try to rewind the clock. She'd been hurt by him. Not physically, but a deep emotional wound that had taken a long time to heal. She knew part of that had been because of what she'd been dealing with at the time with her dad. But it didn't make the hurt any less real.

But Wade… Well, he had hurt her in ways that had taken years of therapy to get past.

More importantly, she had Brody to think about. He had to come first, no matter what. She couldn't risk dragging him into something that could turn into as much of a disaster as the last time around.

Not that Misha would even be open to that. Nor should he. Especially as Brody's doctor.

With a sense of regret, she pulled her hand free under the guise of picking up her glass of water and downing a big sip, welcoming the icy splash as the liquid hit her stomach. It also helped clear her head. "Rather than me telling you about Brody— as a person—I'll let him tell you about himself. He's really a great kid. Despite my mistakes and missteps."

She didn't voice what those were, but Misha was a big boy. He'd understand what she'd left unsaid.

He nodded. "Okay, I'll let Brody tell me what he wants me to know. And I'm sure you need to get back to work soon."

She realized her pulling away hadn't gone unnoticed. There was an aloofness to him in the way he now sat. In the impersonal words he'd just said.

"I do." She hesitated before trying to at least say what she should have said earlier. "And Misha…thank you for agreeing to see him. For considering doing the surgery."

"Of course. I'll let you eat in peace now."

With that, he stood up and walked away, leaving her with an uneasy feeling that she had somehow thrown what was a nice gesture—an attempt to build some kind of bridge between them—back in his face. But she wasn't sure how to undo it, or if she even should. Maybe aloof was good. Maybe it would save her some heartache in the end. She couldn't want something that wasn't offered to her, right?

So she just had to make sure he didn't offer.

As if he would. From all appearances, he was as over her as she was over him.

Ha! Except right at this moment, she wasn't quite sure that she was. Wasn't so sure that her heart wasn't rebuilding the bridge between them that she'd burned down fifteen years ago. And if it succeeded in spanning the gulf between them, then she was in trouble. Big, big trouble. And she might even jeopardize having Misha as Brody's doctor. So she needed to concentrate on that right now. Not on herself. Or her feelings. But on the reality staring her in the face: If Misha wouldn't do this surgery and if she couldn't find someone else in time, then her son might very well pay the price for her own stupidity.

Brody looked just like her.

Taller than his mother, he had sandy blond hair that was a little on the longish side and a smile that tilted up on the right side, just like Lyndsey's.

"So you're Brody. I'm Dr. Lukyanov, but you can call me Misha."

The boy hopped up on the exam table without him asking and smiled. "My mom says you used to go to the same high school."

Misha had wondered if she'd tell her son anything about their past. It looked like she had, but she'd left out the fact that they'd once been crazy about each other. Although it seemed like she'd been able to leave those memories behind easier than he had. Besides the woman in New York that he'd been involved with, he'd also dated a woman in Belarus once he realized Lyndsey had been serious about never having contact with him again. But the relationship had been more physical than anything, and when she'd pressed for more, he ended things. A year later, he'd found himself going through the process of emigrating once again from his home country. He'd thought about reconnecting with Lyndsey. But he'd been certain she'd be married with children. And he'd been right. Although she wasn't married any longer, since her last name was no longer Marshall, she and Wade had been husband and wife for a time.

Misha was in no hurry to form an attachment like that. In truth, after Lindsey, he'd never quite met anyone special enough to consider marriage. And he was happy to keep things that way.

"So, Brody, what kinds of things do you like to do?"

He expected him to say he played sports. He may have looked like Lyndsey, but his physique was like his father's.

"I'm actually in band in school. And some friends and I formed our own band. We meet in one of their garages. I play keyboard and sing backup."

Music. Okay, that was something he hadn't expected. But it explained why Lyndsey didn't want to go the cochlear implant route. Her earlier words about his natural hearing made perfect sense now.

He sat on his stool and tapped his otoscope on his knee. "I'll have to come hear you at one of your gigs."

He immediately regretted saying that.

But only because it was Brody. What he'd told Lyndsey was true. He did try to see his patients as people. And it was something he might have said to any of his patients. But somehow it was different this time. And he wanted to tread carefully.

Brody grinned, that lopsided smile making something tighten in Misha's chest. "We're not quite there yet, but we do have friends over that listen to our jam sessions. You're welcome to come out."

Lyndsey quickly intervened. "I'm sure Misha—er Dr. Lukyanov—is pretty busy with his patients."

If he treated Brody differently than he would his other patients just because of his and Lyndsey's past relationship, then maybe he should rethink taking him on. No. He was going to do exactly what he would have, had Lyndsey been a complete stranger.

"I'm sure I could find a half hour or so to come out and hear you. It'll give me a better idea of your goals for your hearing."

Brody's smile faded. "The thought of not being able to play anymore…of not being able to hear tones and notes…" A muscle worked in the boy's cheek. "It kills me."

The tightness squeezed harder.

"I'm going to do my best to make sure that doesn't happen. I'm going to examine you, but I've gone over all your tests, and it looks like your other ENT has been very thorough." He paused. "Did your mom explain what the surgery we've been discussing entails?"

"Yes. It's kind of like a heart bypass. Only instead of the heart, you'll be bypassing one of the bones in my ear." Brody's eyes met his, and for the first time, Misha saw a hint of fear in the boy's expression.

"Yes, that's a good analogy."

"Will it work?"

Misha's free hand gripped the other end of the otoscope. "I can't make any hard and fast promises. But I'm hopeful that it will."

"Me too."

A few minutes later, Misha completed his exam and rang a tuning fork, pressing it to the bony region just behind Brody's right ear.

"Can you hear that?"

"Kind of."

He repeated the process on the left side of his head. "How about now."

"Yes. That one is a lot better."

"How much better would you say?"

"About fifty percent. On the other side, I'm not sure if I'm just imagining the sound or if I'm actually hearing it."

Misha felt rather than saw Lyndsey's fingers curl into her palms, and she inched her chair closer to her child, a sign of protection that he had seen in many of his patients' parents. But there was something different about the way she did it.

His father is no longer in the picture.

He mentally heard her voice when he'd asked about Brody's dad. Was his absence due to apathy on Wade's part? Or was it something else? Was there some reason Lyndsey didn't want Brody to have any contact with his dad?

Her hand going to her neck during the treatment of the car accident victim came back to him. It had seemed like such an odd reaction for a medical professional to have.

Speculating would get him nowhere,

though, and really the reason for Brody's dad not being around was none of his business.

The teen's voice shook him from his thoughts.

"So what's the next step?"

He was mature. More mature than Misha would have expected. He didn't wait for his mom to ask the hard questions, he was asking them for himself. A testament to Lyndsey's parenting skills.

"The next step is we talk about your goals, which is why I'd like to hear your band. But I also want to show you a short video of how the bypass surgery is done, if you're up for it?"

"Definitely. Can we do it now?"

Misha smiled. "I was hoping you'd say that. I just so happen to have already cued the video on the monitor behind me."

"Great."

Picking up the remote, he pressed play and watched the video he'd seen many times. Except Misha wanted to view it through the eyes of his patients. They were the ones who would ultimately decide if the risk was worth it. Brody had already answered that question. For him, it was definitely worth it.

And for a musician, Misha could definitely appreciate why.

The video showed how the stapes would be separated from the other two bones of the middle ear and carefully removed, leaving its footplate in place. Then a prosthesis would be measured and fitted onto the footplate and attached to the bone next to it. The ultimate goal was for the graft to take over what the stapes—in its undamaged form—would have done.

When the two-minute video finished, Brody released a breath. "Cool. So I'll be able to hear as good as I used to?"

"Maybe not quite as good, because there's been some damage. But it should be measurably better than it is right now. I daresay you'll notice a difference afterward."

"How soon can I have it done?"

"I'm going to look at my schedule and see where the best slot is. I don't want to try to squeeze you in just to get it done quickly. I need to give myself enough time to be meticulous." He squeezed the boy's hand. "You can understand why. I'm going to say it'll be three weeks at least."

"Three weeks. I thought maybe it would take months." The kid smiled. "Thank you. My mom and I appreciate this so much."

Lyndsey spoke up for the first time since they had arrived. "Yes, we do. So much."

He wondered if Brody even knew his mom was working in his department. Well, if he didn't, Misha was sure not going to say anything about it. And it was a relief that she'd only told the boy that they'd simply known each other in high school. That way there'd be no expectations either positive or negative on Brody's side. He didn't want the kid picturing some Hallmark movie moment and trying to play matchmaker.

They wrapped up the appointment, and he told them to have the front desk schedule another appointment for next week, when they would start talking dates and specifics. He also asked if they would give him some idea of when Brody's band would be playing and he would let them know if or when he'd come by to hear them. In the meantime, he would have his office contact their insurance company to start the ball rolling on getting the surgery preapproved.

Misha could only hope he could keep things on his end going just as smoothly. Like not letting his past relationship with Lyndsey influence his decisions with Brody. He'd told him the truth. That he needed to be meticulous in performing the surgery, and if there were any reasons why he couldn't, he would have to hand him off to another surgeon.

But Misha didn't want to do that. And he had no idea why. To make up for hurting her when he'd told her the news that he was returning to Belarus? Lyndsey had obviously gotten over it, so why was he still thinking about it?

He had no idea. But it was time—way past time, actually—to put what had happened between them behind him. Once and for all.

CHAPTER THREE

LYNDSEY HANDED MISHA the list three days later. It was the first time she'd seen him since their appointment and Brody had asked her every night if she'd given it to him yet. If she had her way, the ENT would have as little contact with her son as possible. But she did understand why he wanted this small peek into Brody's life. The nurse in Misha's office had told her how lucky she was to have Misha taking her son's case. She already knew how lucky she was. What might not turn out to be so lucky was working in the same department as the surgeon. But there was no way she was going to make any kind of change before the surgery. She didn't want to do anything that might jeopardize that. If she requested a transfer right now, she was pretty sure he would question it. Might even question if he was the right person to be performing the surgery.

"Thanks, Lynds. I'll let you know which of these I can make."

His shortened use of her name was a remnant of their past, and it made her tummy shiver in a way that was all too familiar.

Could she stay?

She had to. At least for now. She took her commitments seriously and she'd heard the hospital was short on nursing staff, so to move to a different medical center now seemed totally selfish. And despite Misha saying he would never hold someone accountable for something they couldn't control, she couldn't be sure he wouldn't drop the case if she did leave. Or pass it to someone else.

She was almost positive he wouldn't. But almost wasn't good enough. She would stay here for as long as necessary. And after Brody's surgery?

She still believed in doing the best job she could no matter what the circumstances.

Realizing Misha was standing there waiting for some kind of response, she shook the thoughts away. "Okay, thanks." She swallowed before asking the next question. "I know you told Brody he probably wouldn't get all of his hearing back, but can you give me any idea about how much of an improvement we can expect?"

"I won't really know until I see how much ossification there is, and how much cleanup I have to do after getting the stapes out. But if everything goes according to plan, he could get up to eighty percent."

She closed her eyes and breathed a prayer of thanks. "That's good. Better than I'd hoped."

"There's always the chance of complications, so let's adopt a wait-and-see approach once the surgery has been done.

"That makes sense."

Misha folded the slip of paper and slid it into the pocket of his jeans. Black jeans. Jeans that fit his form far too well. She bit her lip and looked away.

Trying to redirect her thoughts, she said, "I looked in on our trach patient a little while ago. It looks like the swelling is starting to recede and they'll be able to reverse the procedure. And the baby is still doing great."

His head tilted. "Is she on our floor? I understood she'd been moved to obstetrics."

Oops. "She was. I…um…went to see her."

Unexpectedly, the corners of his mouth turned up. One of the few times she'd seen him smile since she'd come to work, and this time it was aimed squarely at her. The change in his face was stunning. Her tummy shiver turned into a shudder that was probably visible.

Oh, God. Not good, Lyndsey.

"I'll let you in on a little secret. I went to see her too."

"You did?"

His smile faded. "Is that so surprising? That I would care for my patients?"

"No. Of course not." She found she mourned the loss of his smile more than she should have. "I just thought with how busy you are, you might not have time to follow up on cases that were transferred to another department."

"Sometimes it's not a matter of having time, it's a matter of making time. I do my best not to overschedule myself."

"But I'm sure like other hospitals, Louisiana Southern has quotas you'll have to meet."

He gave a half shrug. "Yes, they have them. But they agreed to give me the time I feel I need. It was one of the conditions I made when I agreed to come here."

Or he wouldn't work for them. He didn't say it, but he didn't have to. And the hospital probably couldn't afford to lose a prestigious surgeon, and Misha knew it. Wow. She already had respect for him as a skilled surgeon. But she found she now respected him as a person. Just like she used to. And Lyndsey probably couldn't afford to think of him in terms of anything other than a surgeon. But it was hard. So hard.

And those damned black jeans kept catching her eye and making her gaze venture to places it shouldn't. Places she'd been before. Places where love and ecstasy could walk hand in hand.

No. Do not think about that. Especially not right now.

She pulled the conversation back to the patient. "Any idea when she'll be able to get the trach reversed?"

"As soon as the swelling goes down enough. Maybe another four or five days. She's still got four weeks until her due date, so they're going to try to keep that baby in place as long as possible."

"So they won't do reconstructive surgery on her trachea right now?"

"They don't think it'll be needed. Surprisingly, it's intact, when by all accounts it should have been crushed."

Something in his phrasing rolled around in her head, trying to find a place to land. Like a pesky insect, she swatted it away before it could. Because she was afraid she might somehow apply it to her and Misha's breakup.

Because it was a completely different thing. Their relationship had been crushed. Destroyed, actually. No part of it remained intact. And if by some weird accident there was something left, she would have to make sure it didn't have a chance to do anything except linger in her subconscious.

"Well, I'd better go look in on my patients," she said.

"Okay, I'll get back to you on the dates. Is the address on here, or do they meet somewhere different each practice?"

"No, it's on there. Brody made sure of it."

For some reason it was important for her to stress that this was Brody's doing and not hers. She did not want him to think that she was eager to see him outside of work.

She could opt not to be at whatever practice Misha chose. Except she drove Brody to practice and normally waited there for him. Sometimes in the garage, where friends normally gathered to hear the group, or in her car. But if she opted for sitting in the car, Misha would think it was because of him.

And it would be. Lyndsey did not want him to know that he still affected her on a physical level, even if it no longer reached her emotions.

At least she hoped it didn't.

Surprisingly, it's intact, when by all accounts it should have been crushed.

No. It was definitely crushed. She remembered that day as clearly as if it were yesterday.

And she was not planning on letting anything "uncrush" it.

Misha sat next to Lyndsey on a folding chair in the humid night air. The band was tuning up in preparation for practice, and there were seven other young people who were either up by the band talking with its members or sitting in a cluster talking among themselves. He felt slightly out of place, but Lyndsey said she regularly sat in on their sessions. When Brody spotted him, he came out from behind the keyboard and walked over to shake his hand. "Thanks for coming. We cover a lot of groups, so hopefully you'll recognize some of the songs."

"I'm sure I will."

It didn't really matter. He'd come to see

what Brody's passion was. He'd done it with some of his patients in New York, too. Not as a guide to whether or not they were worthy of surgery, but as a guide to what surgical candidates hoped to get out of whatever procedure was being considered.

Five minutes later, the band started playing in earnest, and true to what he'd said, the first number was something from the nineties and Misha did recognize it. "The Stillness of Love" was something he remembered hearing on the radio as he and Lyndsey sat in his car and talked about their dreams for the future. They'd joked about the number of children they each wanted, and Lyndsey had laughed when he'd claimed he wanted fifteen. Instead, he had none.

He glanced to his side to see that Lynds had her hands clasped tightly in her lap and was holding herself stiffly erect. She wasn't moving in time with the music or tapping her foot.

Because she too remembered that night? It was the first time they'd made love, parked next to the river in the dark with no one around. But it hadn't been the last. Not by a long shot. If she'd gotten pregnant by him, would he have opted to stay in the States rather than leave with his parents?

But she hadn't. And it would have placed him in the untenable position of choosing his dad's cancer battle over a possible child. He could only thank God that he hadn't had to make that choice. But the choice he had made was just as terrible. His dad, or a love that might or might not last? In the end, he couldn't help but think he'd made the only decision he could have under the circumstances.

Damn. He wasn't even sure why he remembered the song, or why it stirred up all those old memories. Maybe coming here was a mistake. But surely Lyndsey had heard them play this song before, so it wouldn't have taken her by surprise like it had him.

Or maybe she'd even forgotten this was one of the songs on the radio that night.

Then the notes faded away, and he found himself sagging in relief. The band started its next number, and thank God it wasn't anything he recognized. Lyndsey too seemed to have relaxed, her hands no longer clenched together. And this time, her foot was tapping to the beat of an upbeat rock number. So maybe she did remember.

He forced himself to concentrate on Brody.

The band was actually good. Better than Misha had expected them to be. He understood why Lyndsey had pushed so hard for him to have the surgery. If Brody were his, he would have done exactly the same thing.

But he wasn't his. And he needed to keep some semblance of objectivity, or he would be in trouble. And so would Brody.

Worse, he found he liked having Lyndsey sitting next to him as the group moved from one song to the next. If things hadn't turned out the way they had, they might have still been together. Married. With at least one or two children.

But they weren't. And if he had it to do all over again, he still would have gone with his parents. He'd made his decision. And Lyndsey had made hers.

They were the people they were today because of those decisions. Misha had to believe he'd done the right thing.

And not contacting Lyndsey? Respecting her wish for him to leave her alone, had that been the right decision?

But if he had, would she have still chosen Wade over him?

He would never know the answer to that. And in truth, maybe Lyndsey didn't even know the answer to that question.

And dissecting the past wasn't going to change it. So he decided to just take this moment for what it was and enjoy the band's music. And allow himself to enjoy Lyndsey's presence.

Why the hell not? It wouldn't change anything between them. But he could still like sitting here with her, just like he would with any other friend or acquaintance.

It didn't matter that she was neither friend nor acquaintance. She was something else. Something he didn't have to define or categorize.

So he let the music wash over him,

watching Brody put his heart into each note he played.

And he knew that whether he wanted to or not, he was going to be the one to perform that surgery. And he was going to do his damnedest to make sure he gave that boy every ounce of hearing that he possibly could.

When the group finished playing, Brody hurried over to them, his face alight with energy and exhilaration. "So what did you think?"

Misha could honestly answer that question. "I think you guys are phenomenal. And you might not have any paid gigs right now, but if you keep playing the way you do, you will. It won't be long."

"You really think so?"

"I do."

"Our goal is to be a part of the big music festival in Gerard Park."

Misha's head tilted. "I think I remember someone mentioning that festival. You said it's big. How big is it?"

"You mean you've never heard of it?"

Had he? Maybe. But if so, he hadn't paid

attention to announcements about it. He'd been so caught up in his work in the short time he'd been at the hospital that he hadn't gotten out very much. By the time he got home, he was pretty much wiped. In fact, this was the first "outing" he could remember going to in ages. Even in New York, he'd been driven and focused, finding very little time to do much outside of work.

"I guess I must have, but I've never been."

"You have to go, doesn't he, Mom? It's like *the* thing in Lafayette. I've been a bunch of times, and we live an hour away from there."

Since it had taken him almost an hour to get from the hospital to where Brody's band was playing in Centerville, he could see how the festival would have to be good to be worth traveling that far to see it. He glanced at Lyndsey. "Do you commute from here to Lafayette every day to get to work?"

She nodded. "I don't want to move if I don't have to. Brody loves his school, and he might have to give up his band if we moved closer."

And yet she'd been working at the hospital for a year. That was a long time to wait. So why hadn't she looked for something closer to home. Maybe because Lafayette was so much larger, she felt she would have a better chance of finding help for Brody through whatever contacts she made there. And after his surgeries, would she take a job closer to home?

It might be easier for him if she did, but there was a part of him that gave a funny lurch at the thought of it. And yet he'd moved an ocean away from her. It had hurt to do, but he'd been so focused on his dad that he hadn't really thought as much about Lyndsey's hurt as maybe he should have. Then again, he hadn't been able to think much beyond the crisis his family was going through at the time. To expect her to wait would have been living in a fantasy world.

She'd done the right thing in moving on. It just stung that she'd done so as quickly as she had.

Honestly, he had no right to ask her what her plans were. But to drive over an hour every day to get to work and another hour to get home? It was taking time that she could have spent with her son. And yet it was Brody who drove all her decisions. If he were a father, he imagined he would move heaven and earth to get his child the help they needed.

"I can understand that. It's a big leap. Especially when you have someone else to think about."

"Yes. It is."

He thought he heard a hint of irony in her words, although he could have imagined it. Looking at it from her perspective, he could see that being the one left behind was harder than being the one who left, although at the time, he'd placed them on even footing.

Brody chose that moment to break in. "Why don't you come with us to the festival. It starts next week, and we always just buy tickets at the gate. That way you can see what it's like."

Lyndsey's eyes went wide. "Brody. You can't just try to force people to join us."

There'd been no forcing involved. It had been a simple question from a teen who was eager to share something he was passionate about. And somehow, Misha didn't want to disappoint him by turning him down.

"I think I might be able to manage it, depending on what day it's on." He would just have to make sure it didn't interfere with any of his surgical cases, which were on Mondays and Fridays. The rest were appointment days at his office, which was connected to the hospital.

"Brody, why don't you go say goodbye to your friends while I talk to Misha for a minute."

The boy looked from one to the other, before shrugging and moving away from them.

Then Lyndsey turned to him. "You don't have to go just because he asked you to, you know."

"I do know. But I've never been to the festival. Hell, I'm not sure I've even heard of it before he mentioned it. Was it here back when we were dating?"

"Of course. And there's no way you can live in Lafayette and not know about the festival. Most of the literature is written in French Creole. It's a celebration of Cajun culture."

He shook his head. "I haven't been living here all that long."

"So you've seriously never been? Not even with your folks when they lived here?"

"Not even then."

Lyndsey actually laughed before she swallowed the sound. "Seriously, though. You don't have to go."

"Do you want to use the word seriously a few more times?"

"Jerk."

The word made him blink. Their back and forth reminded him of old times. Times that he found he missed more than he realized. Suddenly he wanted to go. Not because he expected to ever get back together with Lyndsey, but he wanted to see it through her eyes. Through Brody's eyes.

And since he'd never been, who better to enjoy it with than people who went to it every year.

"Will it bother you if I join you for the festival?" If she minded, he would back off. But if she didn't…

Then he would go with no expectations other than to enjoy something different.

"No, it's okay. Although I'll warn you that Brody will probably provide a running commentary the entire time. He's passionate about music. And the festival. Just like I'm passionate about his ability to hear."

He wasn't sure it was a good idea. But right now with her beside him, he found he wanted to be with her away from the hospital. Where conversations didn't just revolve around patients and conditions. Where they could just…talk.

And not about their past. Just about life. And what she'd done over the past fifteen years. What had made her choose nursing as a profession. And what had ended her marriage to Wade.

Hmmm…that was really none of his business. If he went, he wasn't going to bring the man up. Not even once. Besides, he didn't know what Brody knew or didn't know about his dad.

"Since I know nothing about the festival, a running commentary will be welcomed."

Lyndsey laughed again, and the sound filled him with a warmth the surprised him. A warmth from the past that threatened to leak into the present.

"Well, don't say I didn't warn you."

"I would never say that." He paused. "Do I need to pack a lunch, or will they have food there?" Some of the festivals in Belarus had concession stands and some were just open air where you brought a blanket and a picnic lunch and enjoyed the company of family and friends.

"Lots of typical foods, and regular things like hot dogs for those who prefer simpler fare."

"I'm not sure how anyone can prefer hot dogs."

She smiled. "That's right. You were never a fan of them at the ball games in high school."

"Not American hot dogs, no. Ours are

more of a kielbasa, and it's what I grew up eating. They just taste completely different to me."

"I'll have to try one sometime."

"Maybe I'll make you one, sometime." When she smiled again, he realized this conversation was taking a turn he didn't want it to take. It was better to keep things on more impersonal footing. Especially since he would be taking on Brody's surgery.

So while he didn't retract his offer, he did steer the conversation back toward more professional footing, and when Brody came back after a few minutes, he'd already said his goodbyes to Lyndsey. He did the same with Brody, then he got the hell out of there.

Before he could change his mind and set a date to cook up one of the most famous Russian comfort foods: sliced kielbasa fried up with potatoes.

CHAPTER FOUR

"I DON'T KNOW if you heard. Joanna went home today."

Misha had stopped by the desk to check on a patient's chart, and Lyndsey blurted out the first thing she could think of.

"Joanna?"

"Our trach patient."

His brows went up. "That's great news. I meant to check on her yesterday, but one of my surgeries ended up more complicated than I expected."

She tensed, hoping she would never hear those words in reference to Brody. "Did it come out okay?"

"I'm hoping. We did a graft over a perforation, and the skin we harvested from the patient ended up being too delicate and came apart. The second attempt held.

We're hopeful it'll take." He paused. "Anyway, I'm glad she was able to go home."

"Me too. They extubated her yesterday afternoon and she was able to breathe on her own, despite some residual edema. But that should go down on its own over the next several days and she and the baby were deemed stable enough to be released."

"That is good news." Misha's light brown hair looked mussed, like he'd run his fingers through it one too many times. She could remember many a time where she'd been the one who'd dug her fingertips into that thick hair during a make-out session and had to smooth it back down before she got out of the car, hoping no one would guess what they'd been up to.

Only she was no longer allowed to run her palms over that sexy head or kiss the tip of his nose when she was done.

Had he had another difficult case today?

"I thought so too." She glanced at where he was struggling to locate something on the computer. "Who are you looking for?"

"Max Sheffield. He has a suspicious lesion on his vocal cord, and I wanted to go in and get a biopsy of it today. But I wanted to look at his scans again, first."

Lyndsey sat down in the chair next to where he stood, only realizing afterward that it put her dangerously close to him. So close that she could smell the clean scent of his soap and a hint of whatever shaving cream he'd used that morning.

Forcing her attention to the screen in front of her, she typed in the name. Nothing came up, so she edited the spelling to Maxwell Sheffield. The entry popped up immediately. "Here it is."

Misha leaned down to look as she scrolled through the screens until she arrived at the scans of the patient's vocal cords. His hair brushed her cheek, making her shiver. The last time she was this close to him, she was kissing him, and he was...

Her whole body tightened in remembered anticipation.

What was wrong with her?

He grabbed a Post-it pad and pen as if he felt no different than he did with any other nurse and jotted down a few notes. "Got it, thanks."

He'd moved on a long time ago. She thought she had too, until he'd brought the past roaring back to taunt her. So not fair.

Trying to nurse the sting, she nodded. "No problem."

When he looked at her, though, his blue irises were darker than they normally were, and as he stood quickly his shoulder accidentally brushed across her breast, causing the nipple to tighten and gooseflesh to ripple across her skin.

Desperate to find something to say that would distract her senses, she blurted out, "I'll check with Brody when I get home about the music festival dates."

Ugh! Reminding him about that wasn't a good ploy. In fact, she was wondering how good of an idea it was for him to go with them. But she couldn't retract the words, and right now she just wanted him to move away from her before her system went into critical meltdown and he noticed how hot and bothered she'd become.

"Feel free to text me once you know."

Text him. Good idea or not? Probably not. But it was way better than calling him and having to listen to that low, smooth voice pour its magic over her.

Oh, jeez, working with him was going to be a disaster if she couldn't get herself under control. And it wasn't like he was trying to do anything. He wasn't. And he definitely wasn't Wade, who she'd found out had tried to hit on her best friend Brittany a few months after they'd gotten married. By then, she was six months pregnant and Wade's college football scholarships hadn't materialized like he'd hoped and he wasn't working. They were living in a camper and things between them were spiraling downhill fast. And to hear that he'd propositioned a friend... She'd confronted him, realizing too late that there were crushed beer cans littering the floor and a college game on TV. Not a good combination. Wade had stood and grabbed her before she could get away. He let her know in no uncertain terms that she was never to question anything he did. And never ever to interrupt him during a game.

Somehow she'd clawed her way free of him before he was able to make her lose consciousness and had fled the camper with the clothes on her back and a fresh set of bruises around her neck.

But at least she'd been alive. And she hadn't lost Brody.

The memory made her throat tighten for a split second and she took a wheezing breath. She quickly righted it. But it was too late. Misha was now looking at her with concern on his face.

"Are you okay?"

"Fine. I was just suppressing a cough."

"I don't think so. Tell me what's going on."

She hesitated, fighting the tiny voice inside of her that told her to tell him everything. But how could she? Despite the fact that she knew none of it had been her fault, there was still a part of her that was embarrassed she'd gotten into the relationship at all. And damn it, it was no one's business. She would choose who she told. And when. She gritted her teeth and stood. "I'm fine. And if that's all you wanted, I have a few patients to check in on."

Good going, Lynds. Use the same excuse

you did last time when you wanted to escape his eagle eyes.

"Is one of them Max?"

What could she say? No? It was pretty obvious he would have been on her list of patients to check.

"As a matter of fact, it is."

"Mind if I head over there with you? I'd like to get a fresh set of vitals, and since I don't see Jacelyn anywhere around, maybe you could assist. I'm just going to give him a local and go in with the endoscope and swab the area. Pathology should pick up any suspicious cells when they go over it."

Did she have a choice? Obviously not, since she couldn't think of an excuse under the sun that would keep her out of that patient's room. Other than *you still affect me more than you should.* And there was no way she was going to admit that to him. Not today. Not ever.

"I don't mind." What was one little white lie among ex-lovers?

Too bad she didn't affect him the same way.

Or did she? He'd gotten up from his chair

pretty quickly back at the desk. She'd been so stuck on her own physical reaction to him that she hadn't had time to analyze that until right now.

Somehow that made it better. Or at least it made her feel better to pretend that was the case.

And when she went to move past him, he took a step back.

Okay. Maybe she wasn't crazy after all. With a jolt of fresh confidence, she walked ahead of him, allowing her hips to tip maybe a little more than usual as she went, although she'd never been very good at trying to have a sexy walk. She normally ended up feeling more like a penguin, making Misha laugh back in the day.

Of course that had been back when she'd been able to laugh at herself too. She tempered her pace and ordered her hip movements to settle down to a normal rhythm. They made it down the short corridor with no incidents, and when they went into the room, they found the thirty-eight-year-old patient reading a book, looking completely at ease. When he saw them, he closed it and set it on the nightstand beside him.

It was rare to find a patient quite so blasé about a possible cancer diagnosis, although Lyndsey knew people could bury their feelings so deep that others had no idea what they were going through. Hadn't she done that with Wade? Pretended life was fine when it was really a train wreck she'd felt she couldn't escape from?

Misha stepped forward. "I'd like to get a little swab from that area we talked about. Are you okay with doing it now?"

"Yep." Max folded his hands in his lap, looking totally at ease, even sending them both a smile that was wider than it should have been.

Misha sent her a look. He'd noticed it too.

He leaned closer and looked in the man's face. "Mr. Sheffield, have you taken something?"

The man scratched his neck and shrugged. It was then that she saw where Misha was headed with his question.

"I took a valium to help me relax, just in case."

"Is it your prescription or someone else's?"

"Mine." He pulled a bottle from his pants pocket and handed it to Misha, who studied it carefully before handing it back. "You should have checked with me first. Some medications can react with the spray I'll use to numb your throat. Fortunately, valium isn't one of them. Did you just take one?"

"I did. Sorry, Doc."

Misha sighed, obviously not happy with his patient, but he went about his preparations, directing Lyndsey where to find some of the equipment he would use. She wasn't trained as a surgical nurse, but she had helped with routine endoscopies before.

She sprayed the back of the patient's tongue with the anesthetic and waited for it to take effect.

"I normally do this in my office, but since you were already in the hospital for another procedure, I thought we could just do it here rather than have you make another appointment at my practice."

He began to feed the endoscope down as they watched its progress on a nearby monitor. "Entering the vocal folds now."

Lyndsey saw the area immediately. It was red and irritated, but not very large at all. Misha saw it too, and readjusted his equipment so that he could rub a special swab across it to collect a specimen.

It took less than five minutes and when he pulled the scope out, the man seemed even more relaxed than he'd been when they arrived. She could see why Misha was irritated with him. But he'd kept his cool better than she might have, simply placing the swab in a collection tube for the pathologist to process.

"Okay, Max, that should do it. Do you have someone to pick you up?"

He nodded. "My brother is down in the waiting room. He'll take me home." There was a slight hoarseness to his voice that she'd noticed earlier. Probably why he'd been referred to Misha.

Misha motioned her to the side and in a

low voice said, "Could you call down there and make sure he's telling the truth. I don't want him on the road like this."

She agreed and went over to Max. "Can you tell me your brother's name and I'll have him come up?"

"Gary. Gary Sheffield."

"Okay, I'll be back in a minute."

She went out to the nurses' desk and called down to the main waiting room. Gary Sheffield was indeed there and was on his way up to their floor to collect his brother. She gave a sigh of relief and went back to the room, giving Misha a quick nod. "He'll be here in a minute."

"Good." Placing his hand on the man's shoulder, he said, "I've printed off instructions for aftercare. Try to rest your voice as much as possible tonight. If you start coughing up any blood, call my office immediately and they'll get in touch with me. For anything more serious, dial 911. Understand?"

Max smiled again. "Perfectly, Doc."

Misha muttered something in Russian before nodding at him. "I'll wait for your brother outside. Lynds, could you help him gather his things?"

"I sure can." She grabbed a plastic bag emblazoned with the name of the hospital and put his book and a few other things he'd laid on the table into it, then handed it to the man.

A minute or two later, Misha entered with another man who resembled Max. Only this person was fully in control of his faculties. "I'm sorry. I told him not to take anything before getting the procedure. Obviously, he didn't listen."

She smiled at his obvious frustration.

Then Gary shot his brother a look that could kill.

"They're sending up a wheelchair for him," she said, then added, "It's hospital policy."

"Okay. Thank you for everything." He glanced at Misha. "You'll let us know what the results are?"

"Yes. I should have them in a couple of days. I'll call as soon as I do."

With that, Misha exited the room with Lyndsey close behind.

She eyed him as they walked back the way they came. "Does that happen often?"

"Fortunately, no. But when it does, it infuriates me."

"Really? I couldn't tell." She batted her eyes at him before laughing. "And did I just hear you cuss in front of a patient?"

He smiled as if it had been drawn from somewhere deep inside of him. "Let's let that be our little secret, okay?"

She'd heard him speak Russian many times when they'd been together. Most of the time, it was when he was in the throes of some passionate emotion, whether anger or something a little sexier. And it never failed to pluck just the right notes in her.

He was one of the sexiest men she'd ever known, and when he dragged his fingers through his hair in an effort to shove a few errant locks off his forehead, they fell right back to where they had been and made her smile. She loved his hair. His chin. Almost everything about him.

Except his decision to leave. And that had just about killed her.

But that was a long time ago, and she

needed to push it back in the past where it belonged and leave it there. Along with her anger.

He couldn't change his decisions any more than she could change hers. And in the end, they'd both come through the years a little older and, in Lyndsey's case, hopefully a whole lot wiser.

And that's what she needed to be where he was concerned for as long as he—or she—worked at Louisiana Southern: A whole lot wiser.

Brody's surgical date was set for two weeks from now. But today he was to go to the Cajun Music Festival. The former he was sure about. But the latter? Well, he wasn't positive that pushing to go with Lyndsey and her son was one of his better decisions. And he had a feeling Lynds felt the same way. But what was done was done. And to back out at the last second would look suspicious to Lyndsey and it might upset Brody, who'd really wanted him to come. He wasn't sure why. He'd been nothing but professional with the kid and it needed to stay that way. But then again, Misha held the boy's hearing in his hands, and Brody probably wanted him to see firsthand how important this surgery was to him.

He knew. It was important to Misha too, for a variety of reasons. Some of which were not as smart as others. He wanted to do this for Lyndsey. Maybe to make up for causing her pain all those years ago?

Possibly. But he'd also sensed a hint of sadness in her that he hadn't understood. He had the sense it wasn't directly tied to what had happened fifteen years ago between them. Maybe if he could take this one weight off her shoulders, it would take away that heaviness. At least that was his hope.

They'd agreed to meet at the hospital and go in his car. He figured if they stayed a couple of hours, he would have done his duty, and he could drop them back off at the hospital. It would be easy and painless. At least that was his hope.

When he got to the parking garage, he saw they were already there waiting for him. Great. Late again. This time it wasn't due to a patient, but due to his own reticence about going. He did not need to get attached to the boy.

Or to his mom, for that matter. Standing next to her as she'd looked for Max Sheffield's name had done a number on him, and from what he'd read in her body language, he wasn't the only one who'd felt it. If they'd been alone, he couldn't guarantee that he wouldn't have turned her to face him and looked deeply in her eyes before drawing her closer.

Proklyatiye! Not something he should even be imagining, much less admitting to himself.

"Sorry to keep you waiting." His voice was gruffer than he'd meant it to be and Lyndsey shot him a look.

Brody shrugged. "We just got here, actually. Our car wouldn't start, and Mom had to ask a friend to bring us."

He frowned. "I could have picked you up."

"It's an hour out of your way. I'll just call her when we're done, and she'll come and get us again."

"No need. I'll take you home."

"That's okay, you don't have to—"

"I know I don't have to. But I want to. It will be nice to see Centerville again. I assume it hasn't changed much."

Lyndsey glanced at him, but she didn't smile. "No, it hasn't. But then people seem to like it that way."

"Do they?"

"I think so. They get stuck in the memories of the past and don't want to move beyond them." She bit her lip. "I'm talking about the people who live there. Not me."

"I didn't think you were talking about you." He clicked the button on his fob to unlock the car, and Brody opened the door to the backseat, climbing inside. Misha opened the front passenger door and nodded at Lyndsey. "Go ahead. It's fine."

He then walked around to the driver's side and got in, pressing the button to start the vehicle.

Fifteen minutes later, they were on the grounds of the festival, and Brody had their path all mapped out on a sheet of paper.

"I want you to see it all."

Misha glanced around the venue. It was huge. "I'm not sure that's even possible." But he was impressed by Brody's diligence. Lyndsey had done a wonderful job raising him.

"It's not. But you can at least see a little of everything, starting with some of the Cajun jam sessions. They're this way."

Brody whisked them from space to space. It seemed everything had its own tent or stage. Traditional music, modern, dance, it was all there, along with something for the kids. And food. Hell, the food. He tried a little of everything. The heat levels went from mild to atomic. He was pretty sure he'd just blown a hole in his gut with the last bite of spicy shrimp.

He glanced at Lyndsey. "You do this every year?"

"Every. Year. It's a tradition in our little family of two." She smiled, glancing at Brody with obvious affection and ruffling his hair.

No mention of Wade once again. But then, she'd said he wasn't in the picture. So where was he? Had he moved on to someone else? He did seem the type. The type to up and leave.

Like Misha had done?

That was different. Or so he'd thought back then.

But evidently she'd never remarried, since she still carried the McKinna name. And her ring finger was undeniably empty.

"It's a tradition to stuff yourself full enough to…?"

"Don't say it. I'm struggling to keep a lid on my stomach as it is. I'm glad we're walking."

"You and me both. I should be done digesting things about ten years from now." He sent her a smile. "But I have to admit this was nice. A great tradition you have here, Lynds. You're very lucky, you know."

The words were out before he realized it. But he meant them. She was happy with her "little family of two." It was evident in the shine in her eyes every time she looked at her son. Every time she talked about him.

"Lucky?" She shrugged, looking out over the venue. "I don't know that I'd go that far. It's taken me a long time to get where I am. A very long time. And Brody…he's everything to me. He's why my heart is still beating in my chest."

He turned and looked down at her. "He's a good kid. You should be proud of him."

"I am. More than you can ever know."

Their gazes met. Held. His hand lifted to cup her cheek, then Brody came rushing toward them like a whirlwind. "They've started the last set that I want to see."

Lyndsey, evidently unaware of what he'd been about to do, sent him a shrug. "Brody is being Brody." She might not realize what had almost happened, but he did. And he needed to check himself before he did something he couldn't take back. Something that might change what could—and would—happen in regard to Brody's surgery.

He and Lyndsey followed the boy back to the stage where the jam sessions were being held. Brody was obviously enthralled by everything that was happening on stage.

He glanced at his watch. Wow, they'd been here for almost four hours. That had to be a record for Misha. And he'd had fun. Something he couldn't remember having in a long, long time. Maybe since high school.

That seemed like a lifetime ago, and yet he remembered so much about those days. He'd been so young back then. Impulsive and sometimes stupid. He glanced at Lyndsey before pulling his attention back to the stage. Right now he couldn't afford to be either impulsive or stupid.

The band ended with a long, loud riff that went on for probably ten minutes. And when it ended, people all around them were standing on their feet and clapping and yelling. He couldn't blame them. It had been a workout for both the musicians and the audience, which seemed to throw as much energy into the mix as the band members had.

Brody turned to him. "Did you like it?"

"I really did. Thanks so much for inviting me."

Surprisingly, Brody glanced at his phone. "What time were you thinking of getting back?"

"Whatever time you think." In all honesty, he was ready to go now.

Lyndsey must have read something into her son's words. "Do you have something going on tonight?"

"Me and the boys were going to have a jam session of our own if I got back in time. If it's all right with you, that is."

"It depends on what Misha's plans are." She glanced at him. "I can certainly get Brittany to come out and get us. I know this has lasted longer than you probably thought it would."

There was no way he was going to let her and Brody sit around for an hour waiting on a ride when they could already be home.

"I'll take you home. It's not a big deal."

"Are you sure?"

"Absolutely."

With that decided, they piled back into Misha's car and headed toward Centerville and the end of what had been a very pleasant evening.

CHAPTER FIVE

MISHA PARKED OUTSIDE of Lyndsey's house, a move that felt both familiar and foreign. It had been years since they'd sat in a car together. And of course Brody was there, so it wasn't the same at all.

Before she could exit the vehicle though, Brody leaped out of the car. "I'll be back by nine, okay, Mom?"

"Yes. Nine o'clock for sure, though. Tomorrow's a school day."

A second later, the boy wheeled a bike from the garage, hopped on and was gone, pedaling out of sight.

"He makes my head spin sometimes, I swear." She looked at Misha. "But it's been good to see him smile like that. With the fear about his hearing, it's been a while since I've seen him so carefree. But now that a date for surgery has been set, he's got hope."

They exited the vehicle, and he walked her to the door. "Thanks for tonight," he said. "It was good to get a peek into Brody's passions. I had a good time."

"So did I."

They stood in front of her door. And she couldn't quite bring herself to turn toward it and let herself in. Instead, she leaned back against it and looked at him. He was so damned gorgeous.

Neither of them moved for a long moment. Then her hand slowly lifted and pushed a strand of hair off his forehead, allowing her fingers to trail across his skin as she did. He was so warm, just like he'd been on so many nights in their past. The times when his gentle touch carried her to places she'd only dreamed about. And now they were alone. There was nothing to stop them if they might want to…

"Lynds…" As if he heard her thoughts, he took a step forward, crowding her against the door. Once upon a time that might have startled her. Frightened her, even. But this was Misha. And he would never physically hurt her.

He stared at her for a long moment, then leaned his face toward hers. And suddenly he was doing what she'd longed for him to do. He was kissing her.

The first touch of his mouth to hers was ecstasy. How long had it been since he'd done this?

A lifetime.

How could this be happening?

He moved closer, his body connecting with hers, bringing to life old and familiar nerve pathways that hurried their preparations.

His tongue touched her lips, pushed past them. And she welcomed him inside. Welcomed his touch, his taste. Her fingers found the warm hair at the base of his skull and tunneled deep, relishing the feel of his skull and the warm skin that covered every inch of his body.

It could be hers again. Tonight. Brody wouldn't be home for almost two hours. All she had to do was reach behind her for the doorknob and open the door.

Her hand reached back and found what she was looking for. But instead of turning it, she felt the cold reality of what that would mean.

She'd be opening herself up to be hurt all over again. Misha didn't want promises of forever. She wasn't sure what she was looking for here, but…

No!

Before she could say the word out loud, though, Misha's head came up and he took a step back.

Withdrawing.

And the loss… She didn't want to feel it again. But it was already creeping through her. How much worse would it be to get involved with him? This time it wouldn't just hurt her. It could potentially hurt her son as well.

"Lyndsey. This can't happen. For so many reasons."

She bit her lip hard enough to hurt. Hard enough to force her to separate fantasy from reality. And that kiss…was make believe. Even Misha recognized it.

"I know. I've managed to give Brody a stable life after Wade…left."

No. She didn't need to bring her ex-husband into this. "I'm just not willing to risk that again. Not for anyone."

And especially not you.

She didn't say those words out loud. But then again, she didn't have to. His face had already morphed from sexy to closed the moment he stepped back from her.

"I understand. Believe me. I'm not looking to start anything anymore than you are. And if we did, you'd have to find a new surgeon."

"No!" The word exploded from her mouth, and she forced herself to repeat it in a lower tone. "He trusts you. I'm not sure he'll let another surgeon move forward with the surgery. He…he trusts you."

She was repeating herself, but she was desperate not to let what almost happened ruin things for her son. He deserved this chance. "Please don't make us start from scratch."

"I wasn't saying I wouldn't do the surgery. I only meant we have to keep things professional."

"Of course. If anyone has a chance to make Brody's dream a reality, it's you."

He nodded, face unsmiling. "We'll just consider tonight a blip of something from the past that never should have raised its head."

Was it that easy for him to just pull back and forget tonight had ever happened? Evidently. After all, he'd left for Belarus and seemingly forgotten all about her. He'd been in the States for how long now? And never once had he tried to get in touch with her.

Working with him was going to be torture if she couldn't get past this. But she would…somehow.

And once Brody's surgery was over and done, she could make the decision about whether to keep working in his department or request a transfer. Or, once she no longer needed to be at a big hospital, she could go back to a hospital closer to her hometown. Where she never had to see Misha again.

* * *

The next couple of days were hard. Misha found himself avoiding the ENT department of the hospital, except today when he actually had a surgery he couldn't get out of. But what he'd said at her doorstep was true. They could not have a relationship for any number of reasons, but the first and foremost was because of Brody's surgery. Conflict of interest was never a good thing. There was a reason they didn't let doctors treat family members or those closest to them.

As he rounded the corner, hoping to avoid the nurses' station, he spotted a familiar face. He just couldn't place who she was.

But when she saw him, she stopped in her tracks, a frown appearing out of nowhere.

"Misha?"

He was still struggling to place her when she shook her head. "Lyndsey told me you were working here, that you were going to do Brody's surgery." Her mouth twisted.

"But I was hoping I'd never have to lay eyes on you again."

He was taken aback by her sudden hostility, and then who she was dawned on him. There'd only be one person besides Lyndsey who could be that angry with him. "Brittany?"

"So you do recognize me."

He hadn't. Not until this very second, when he remembered Lyndsey mentioning that Brittany had driven her to the hospital two days ago when they were going to the music festival.

That the woman wasn't his biggest fan was obvious. Back in high school, they'd all been friends. Close friends. But he got it. He'd been the one to walk out on Lyndsey and hurt her. He imagined he didn't have many friends left at that school.

"Lyndsey said you brought her to the hospital when her car broke down. Thanks for that."

"Don't thank me. I didn't agree with Brody inviting you to that festival." Her brows went up. "You know, you're reason

she wound up with that jackass of a husband."

Anger welled up inside of him. "Marry-
ing Wade was her choice. Not mine."

"Her choice? If you knew what he put
her through. God…he almost ki—"

"Brittany! That's enough." Lyndsey's
voice cut through her friend's tirade like
a knife.

Her mouth shut with a snap and she
shook her head. "Oh, honey, I'm sorry."

"It's okay." But Lyndsey's voice was
cool. Cooler than he'd heard it since that
night when he'd told her he was going back
to Belarus.

Brittany looked from her to Misha before moving over to her friend. "I came by
to tell you your car should be ready soon. I
wanted to make sure you were okay." She
seemed to stumble over her words before
finally adding, "And… I'm really sorry."

Lyndsey pulled in a deep breath and
gave her friend a hug. "It's okay. I know
why you did it. But none of that has anything to do with Misha. Those choices were
mine and mine alone."

So why was there a sense of guilt that was suddenly pressing on his chest like a pile of boulders? Because whatever she'd been about to say was something that Lyndsey hadn't wanted him to hear.

That Brittany blamed him for whatever happened with Wade was obvious. Had her ex felt like she'd never gotten over him? Had it driven them apart? She did say he'd left.

Maybe. But that explanation didn't feel quite right. It was as if a very important piece was missing. Without it, the puzzle would never be complete.

But did Misha even have a right to know? Hadn't he given up any right to know anything about Lyndsey's life when he'd left her behind?

Unexpectedly, her friend turned to him. "Listen, I'm sorry. I shouldn't have said that. Any of that. Lyndsey's heart is more forgiving than mine is. And if she chooses not to blame you for…anything, then that's her right. And I'll respect her wishes." She sent him a hard smile. "Just don't expect me to roll out the welcome mat if you ever come back to Centerville."

He was pretty sure that was one mat that no one was going to roll out. The weirdest thing was, they evidently had one thing in common when it came to Wade. It sounded like Brittany wasn't a fan of his either. He'd venture even further to say that she might actually hate the other man even more than she hated him.

Or maybe he was mistaken. All he knew was that Brittany seemed to blame him for everything that had gone wrong in Lyndsey's life after he left.

And the sad thing was, she could very well be right.

Lyndsey couldn't believe that Brittany had almost blurted out the truth about Wade. It was something she'd never even told Brody. Her son did not need that weighing down on him, and she knew him well enough to know he'd find a way to blame himself for it. Or somehow imagine that he might grow up just like his lowlife dad.

Nothing could be further from the truth.

Brody was one of the kindest, most compassionate human beings she'd ever met. Maybe she was biased because he was her son, but she wasn't the only one who felt that way. Look at how he'd included Misha in their little circle at the music festival.

She just wished he didn't seem so attached to Misha. But right now, it was what it was. She was pretty sure it was hero worship over what Misha might be able to do for his hearing. And she wasn't about to let anything or anyone jeopardize him getting that surgery. So she needed to smooth whatever damage Brittany had done, if she could.

Once her friend left with a promise to call her later, she turned to Misha. "I am so sorry about that. She has a big heart."

"I can see that. And it's okay." He paused as if trying to formulate his words with care. He had to have been shocked at how hard Brittany had come at him. "I'm glad you have people like her in your corner. If anyone deserves a friend like that, it's you. And I'm really sorry you had such a hard time in your marriage."

"It's over and done with. And it's something I try my best not to dwell on."

"Brody doesn't know about whatever Brittany was accusing me of?"

She shook her head. "No. And he never will if I have anything to say about it."

Something crystallized in his look that made her want to head him off at the pass. She did not want him asking any more questions about Wade or her marriage. Especially not before Brody's surgery.

"Just know that what Brittany said wasn't really aimed at you."

He smiled. "I'm pretty sure it was. But that's okay. I can take it. And she's probably right in a lot of ways."

"No. She's not. People are responsible for their own choices. And I owned mine a long time ago. That doesn't mean I can't move forward or do the best I know how for Brody. I have done that and I'll continue to do so, as long as these lungs have breath."

And it was because of Brody that she'd given that last huge effort to get Wade off her. And it had worked. Thank God, it had worked.

"I get it."

Maybe that was how he'd felt when he needed to go back to Belarus. That he'd move heaven and earth for his family. Now that she was older, she could see how he might have been torn between staying and going. But he could have told her that. Instead, he'd withdrawn emotionally in a way that she had a hard time doing.

One thing was for sure. He was never going to know the truth about Wade, unless she someday decided she wanted him to know.

But honestly, she didn't see that happening anytime soon. If ever. There was no reason to tell him.

"Anyway, thanks again for understanding. I just wish Brody's surgery was over and done with and that we get the results we're hoping for."

"We only have a week to go, and unless something awful happens, there's no reason why this surgery won't be a success. Brody is young, he's in the beginning stages of otosclerosis, and he's in excellent health. He's the perfect candidate for surgery. Let's just take things one day at a time. And before you know it this will all be over."

A shudder rolled through her. Someone had once said almost that exact same thing as she lay on a hospital gurney praying that her son had somehow survived the attack, that his tiny life was still safe inside of her.

Just go to sleep. And before you know it, this will be all over.

She had. And when she had woken up, she'd instinctively known that Brody was still there. Still alive. And so was she. She was never going to take that for granted again. For anyone. So it was a very good thing that he'd put a stop to that kiss outside of her home. It was a mistake she hoped she'd never make again.

She and Misha had a past, yes. But that didn't mean they had a future. They didn't. And the sooner she realized that, the better.

CHAPTER SIX

MISHA SPOKE TO the woman in tones that he hoped were soothing, but he wasn't the best at doing that. Especially where young children were concerned. And this worried mom was cradling a child around five years old who'd shoved a pencil through his ear. The blood and drainage said he'd perforated his eardrum. The sooner he could look—

Lyndsey pushed through the door, and he gave a sigh of relief. It had been a couple of days since that encounter in the hallway with Brittany, and he could swear Lyndsey had been avoiding him.

And he hadn't minded, especially since that kiss in front of her doorway was still rolling around in his skull toppling over everything in its path. He'd put a stop to it, and it had been the right thing to do. But right now, she was a ray of sunshine in a tense situation. The child did not want Misha looking at his ear and had screamed bloody murder every time he came anywhere near him with his otoscope. And his mom, who he couldn't blame for being protective, wasn't helping matters.

Misha had felt the same way when there'd been a hint that Wade had hurt Lyndsey in some way. He'd felt an anger that had almost consumed him, had made him want to protect her from whatever had happened. Except it was probably all in his imagination. And whatever it was, it had happened a long time ago.

Lyndsey hadn't offered any explanation other than to apologize for Brittany's words. In other words, it was none of his business.

She glanced at him and then at the mom and son duo seated on the exam table and he could almost see the wheels in her head sizing up the situation.

Ignoring him, she went over to the mom and whispered something in her ear. The woman looked at her for a second or two and then nodded. "Okay. You can try. His name is Lucas."

"Lucas. I know your ear hurts right now, but I have something at my desk I think you might like to look at."

The face that had been buried in his mother's chest peeked out at her, his cheeks and nose red from all the crying he'd done. "W-what is it?"

She lowered her voice to a conspiratorial whisper. "An elf on a shelf is living in a drawer at the nurses' desk."

"No there isn't." There was a sniffle, but there was also interest.

"There is. Really. I don't let many people see him." She glanced at Misha. "Dr. Lukyanov has never seen him. But if you promise you won't tell anyone but your mom about him, I might let you peek inside."

"Really?"

"Yes. But you have to promise that afterwards you'll let the doctor look in your ear to see if everything is okay."

Lucas sniffed louder. "Matthew told me to stick my pencil in there. But it hurt, and my mom came and said I had to come here." His small chin wobbled. "But I want to go home."

"And you will. But Dr. Lukyanov can help fix your ear so that it doesn't hurt anymore."

"Lyndsey…" Misha said.

She shot him a look that made him swallow the rest of that sentence. "He has magic drops that can make it stop hurting. Don't you, Doctor?"

Hell, she was talking about his anesthetic drops. But he hadn't even seen the ear yet, had no idea if there was damage to anything besides the ear drum. If the boy had dislocated any of the small bones within that canal, he might need surgery. But she was right. He couldn't do any of that if he couldn't get a look inside. And he really didn't want to have to restrain him to do it, if he didn't have to.

"Yes, I really do have some drops."

The boy glared at him for a minute as if he might be lying. Why in the world did he believe Lyndsey and not him? Because she had that kind of personality. One that drew you in and made you want to trust anything she said.

He'd certainly believed her fifteen years ago when she said they were through.

She held her hand out to Lucas. "Will you come with me and see our elf? His name is Ornament, but we call him Ornery for short."

He lifted his head before putting his hand to his ear and looking at Misha. "You promise you'll make it stop hurting afterwards?"

"I promise."

Lyndsey carefully lifted the boy down from the table and took his free hand in hers. "We'll be right back. No one else is allowed to see Ornery, though. Only Lucas."

In other words, he and the boy's mom were to stay put.

He nodded and held his hand over his heart. "I promise I won't peek."

The pair went through the door and Misha quickly relayed what needed to happen next to Lucas's mom and stressed that she needed to work with him, even if Lucas cried. The longer it went without being looked at, the more chance there was of infection or permanent hearing loss.

"I will. It's just so hard to see him in pain."

"I know. Believe me." It had been awful to see Lyndsey in such pain fifteen years ago, knowing there was nothing he could do about it. Nothing he could change.

"When they come back, I'd like to let Lyndsey assist me—the nurse who took him to see the elf—since he now trusts her. If you don't mind standing a little ways away, it would make it easier for you. And ultimately for him."

"I will. My oldest daughter had to be strapped to a board to let her lip be stitched back together. I had to leave the room. My husband was here then, but he's deployed for the next six months. He knew just what to do."

"And so will you. Just trust that we're trying to help Lucas, not hurt him."

"I do trust you. I'll try to channel my husband."

Less than three minutes later, Lyndsey

opened the door again and led Lucas inside. He had something clutched in his hand this time.

Misha stared at it. "Is that a…candy cane?"

"Not just any candy cane. It came from Ornery and it's magic, right, Lucas?"

The boy nodded, before moaning and cradling his ear. "I can eat it after the doctor looks at my ear. Ornery told Lyndsey that Mommy has to keep it for me until afterwards." His chin wobbled again. "You promise the drops will make it stop hurting?"

"I promise." He glanced at her then back at Lucas. "Why don't you give the candy cane to your mom while Lyndsey gets the drops?"

He did as Misha asked, but when he tried to hold onto her again, she nudged him back toward the doctor. "You have to let him look. You promised Ornery, didn't you?"

He nodded then looked at the instrument in Misha's hand. "Will that hurt? The pencil hurt when I put it in my ear."

"It won't hurt because it doesn't go in very far." He knelt down to be at the same level as the child, holding the instrument out to him. "Here, you can look at it. If you press this button a light comes on. Like a flashlight. It lets me see what's going on inside your ear."

Lucas took the otoscope and pressed the button, watching as the light came on. He pointed it at various objects in the room. "It's cool."

"It is. I bet if Ornery had an earache, he would let me look in his ear."

"That's what Lyndsey said too."

When Misha glanced over at her, he found her clutching the drops, watching him with a weird expression on her face. A softness he hadn't seen in a long time. Something in his stomach shifted and he had to look away, forcing himself to concentrate on Lucas instead. "You can stand right there, if you want, while I look. It might hurt a very little bit because I have to tug a little bit on your earlobe, like this." He chose the unaffected ear to demonstrate on to show how much pressure he would put on it. "First, I'm going to look in this ear, okay?"

Lucas nodded, seeming relieved that he wasn't going to start with the injured one.

"Turn this way a little bit." He had Lucas turn his good ear toward him. "Good."

He used the otoscope to look in the boy's ear. "Everything looks perfect in there. Did that hurt?"

"No."

"Okay, turn the other way."

Lucas hesitated, glancing back at his mom, who nodded at him. Lyndsey came over and knelt next to him. "Here. Hold my hand. Squeeze it as hard as you want."

The boy took her fingers.

Misha showed him the otoscope again. "It'll be the same thing on this ear. It'll just take a little longer because I need to get a very good look at it."

"Okay."

Trying to be as careful as he could, Misha pulled down a bit on the boy's earlobe to open the canal and then looked inside with the otoscope. There was blood and sure enough there was a hole in the tympanic membrane, but it was smaller than it could have been. Probably only the point had penetrated, which was a very good sign. It meant that there'd probably been no damage beyond that point. It should heal on its own. He'd prescribe some antibiotic drops just to ward off any infection from the foreign object, but the drum should heal over without needing to place a patch over it.

He removed the otoscope and sat back. "And that was it."

"Do you need to operate?" Lucas's mom stared at him, the words quivering with the threat of tears.

"No. No operation needed." He couldn't keep his glance from flickering to Lyndsey for a second. Was she wishing that Brody's problem was just as simple to fix?

He shifted his attention to Lucas's mom. "It actually should heal all by itself. It's a very small puncture wound, about this big…" He used his thumb and forefinger to give her an idea of size. "I don't think anything more than the lead went through. But it bled just like any other wound might."

"We don't need to do anything?"

"Nope. I'll give you some ear drops to use for a week. Two drops in the ear, twice a day. If it gets worse or he starts having any kind of discharge from the ear, I want to see him again."

"Thank God."

He looked at the boy. "So how about some of those magic drops now? Do you still want them?"

"Yes."

"And you'll let your mom put the other drops in your ear too? They'll help your ear get all better."

"They won't hurt either?"

"No. They might tickle, but they won't hurt. Mom, if you'll get on the exam table, we'll let Lucas put his head in your lap so I can drop one or two of my magic drops in his ear and help it feel better." Lyndsey's plan had worked like a charm. Maybe because she had a son of her own and had maybe walked some of these same paths with him. Whatever the reason, he was grateful she was in his department and that she was very good at her job.

It took very little effort to get Lucas into position. Misha put a single drop of anesthetic in his ear. "Stay still for just a minute so it can work its magic."

He glanced at his watch and ticked down a minute and a half. "Okay, you can sit up."

Lucas sat up and turned his eyes to Lyndsey first and then Misha. "It worked."

"It doesn't hurt?"

"Not even a little."

Misha smiled. "I'm glad. The magic will wear off after a while and it might start hurting again, but your mom can give you Tylenol and that should make it feel better again." He fixed the boy with a stern look. "Are you going to put anything in your ear again?"

"Nooo." The way Lucas drew the word out made Misha's smile widen.

"That's very good to hear. I think Ornery would be very sad if he heard you'd done something like that again. You can eat your candy cane on your way home, okay?"

He printed off a sheet of care instructions for Lucas's mom and called in a prescription before sending the duo on their way with a sigh of relief.

Lyndsey had worked her magic and he was very glad for it. He only hoped that her magic didn't extend past little boys and their childhood ouchies. But he had a feeling she was even more powerful than Ornery the elf. Misha just had to make sure she had no opportunity to send any of that magic his way. If she did, he might just fall under her spell all over again.

Brody was behind the doors of the surgical suite at this very moment being prepped for his first procedure, and she felt like someone had punched her in the gut. Breaths were hard to come by and her nerves were wound tighter than tight.

Before he'd been whisked away, he'd told her that he'd be fine. But he hadn't said it with his voice. Instead, he'd signed the message to her. Her eyes had been awash with tears as he'd slowly moved his hands to form each word. He'd been learning it just in case worse came to worst and something went terribly wrong with the surgery.

Lyndsey, with fear in her heart, signed back to him for the first time ever. She'd never admitted to him that she'd also been learning sign language—hadn't wanted him to see that she'd ever doubted they'd find help.

She'd hugged him for a long, long time before Misha had gently pulled her away. "I'll let you know as soon as he's done."

And now it was a waiting game. She'd asked if she could view the surgery up in the observation area, but he'd quietly told her no. That it would be a distraction he didn't need, and it would just cause her unnecessary anxiety.

Brittany, who was now seated next to her, gripped her hand. "He'll be okay, honey. He's strong. And from what you've said, Mikhail is an expert in this surgery."

"He is. I'm so lucky he agreed to do it."

Her friend's jaw tightened, but she didn't say anything beyond what she'd already said. It was one of those things on which they'd had to agree to disagree in order to save their friendship. Brittany blamed Misha for everything that had happened to her. But Lyndsey didn't. Not anymore. She had at one time. Had convinced herself that she hated him. But seeing him again? She realized she'd vilified someone who hadn't deserved it. She could see that now, even if Brittany couldn't.

And right now, the very person she'd once thought was the worst human being on the planet was fighting to save her son's hearing. And for that, he was a hero. Her hero. Brody's hero. And she would be forever grateful to him in ways she couldn't explain. And maybe she didn't have to. Maybe she could just accept it for what it was.

A gift. One she didn't deserve, but one that was hanging over her head anyway. She just prayed Misha could pull it off.

Misha's concentration was complete. He couldn't see or think of anything beyond what he saw through his loupes and on the monitor to the right of him.

The stapes, all but its footplate, had been lifted free from its spot, and he was preparing it for the prosthesis. First, he drilled a precision hole in the footplate just large enough to accept the base of what looked like a tiny piston. This microprosthesis would transfer the vibrations that the stapes no longer could.

This was the moment of truth.

He was vaguely aware of someone swabbing sweat from his brow and temples but kept moving forward, trying his damnedest not to screw something up. His hand shifted for a millisecond, and he immediately stopped the drill, breathing a prayer that the size of the opening was correct.

He picked up the prosthesis with the pincers of his tool and slid it into place. It was snug but not too tight. It had to be able to move freely but without slipping through the hole he'd made.

On the other end of the prosthesis was a tiny C-clamp that he laid over the bone next to where the stapes had been and checked its position before pinching the ends of the clamp and securing it in place. He nudged either side of the piston and it had just enough give without falling from its new position. He stood there for a moment racking his brain for anything else he needed to check. But he'd done it all. And for now, it looked like Brody's new prosthesis might just work.

He held his fingers up to no one in particular and crossed them in a sign of hope.

Because that's all he could do right now. Hope. Hope he'd thought of everything. Hope that Brody's body accepted its tiny new addition. And hope that everything would heal exactly as it should. Just like their trach patient had done.

Lindsey's reaction that day still puzzled him. The way her hand had gone to her throat with a convulsive movement. The jolt of fear he thought he'd spotted in her face before she got control over herself. Her reaction afterward when he'd asked her about it.

Brittany's words came back to him. "He almost ki…"

He almost what?

Not again. He didn't need to start going through this again.

He finished up the final steps to surgery, checking things one last time.

There was no reason to think this wouldn't be a complete success.

He blew out a breath to release the tension that had been building inside of him. "Okay. Let's wake him up."

The nursing staff shifted Brody so that he was face up on the bed once again while they reversed the medications that had kept him unaware and comfortable during surgery. Soon, a groggy patient was repeating his own name when prompted.

Misha moved himself into Brody's line of sight. "It looks like everything went as planned. It'll take a little time for everything to heal, but I think it's been a success." He touched the teen's arm. "But no loud music for the next several weeks, okay?"

Brody didn't answer, but he nodded his head. That was a good sign his hearing was no worse. He only hoped there would be a significant improvement. "I need to go let your mom know."

Brody nodded his head again, lids flickering shut and staying there. He probably would remember very little of this conversation. And that was okay. Most of it wouldn't matter.

What would matter, however, was how much hearing Brody had now, and how much he could expect to have in the future. If this procedure was as successful as he'd hoped, there was no reason they couldn't do the same for the boy's other ear, which was in the very initial stages of ossification.

He stripped off his gloves and tossed them in the nearest receptacle, then headed for the waiting room, not bothering to take off his surgical scrubs. When he reached the room, he saw Lyndsey and her friend Brittany leaning over something, their heads close together. When he moved closer, he saw it was an article on Brittany's phone.

The headline blazed out from the screen: *Wade McKinna, High School Quarterback, Released from Prison.*

A million thoughts swept through his mind, but he took a step back and cleared his throat to announce his presence. He hadn't meant to pry, and he now wished he could unsee the headline.

Suddenly, Lyndsey's words about Brody's dad being out of the picture took on new meaning. He'd been literally out of the picture. Not because he'd gotten involved with someone else or had disappeared to a different part of the country. No. The man had been in jail.

For what?

Possibilities swirled in his head in quick succession until all he saw was one probable conclusion. One so terrible he wished he could erase it from his mind.

But right now, he couldn't worry about any of that. He needed to tell Lyndsey that her son's surgery had been a complete success. That's all that mattered at the moment.

Brittany was the first to look up, and she snapped off her screen so fast that Lyndsey glanced over at her before seeing him. Then she sat straight up, eyes widening.

"Brody?"

"He's fine. He's just waking up. He'll be

in recovery for a while, but as soon as he's transferred to a room, you can see him."

Brittany stood. "That's my cue to leave. Unless you want me to follow you home. I totally can."

"No, I'll be okay. I have no idea how long it will take to release Brody. Go home. I'll be fine." When her friend looked dubious, Lyndsey reiterated the words.

"Okay." Leaning down, she gave Lyndsey a kiss on the cheek. "But call me the minute you get home to let me know you made it and are safely inside your house."

Misha's gut tightened. Were they worried about Wade showing up at her house?

"I will. And thank you."

Brittany gave him a look that, while not quite friendly, was definitely less hostile than what he'd experienced the last time their paths had crossed. Then she headed toward the elevator.

"So you think it went well?" The hope in her face sent a spear through his gut. He was beyond glad that he had good news for her, even if it came on the heels of what looked to be bad news.

He forced his mind back to Brody. "Yes. I think it went very well. We'll have to wait a little while to be sure, but I think the surgery was a complete success. It'll take him a little while to adjust to things, and he might have some tinnitus for a bit, but I'm pretty sure he's going to be playing music with more gusto than ever."

"I can't believe it. The last year has been…"

"Hard." He pulled the word out for her.

"Yes. Hard. Harder than I ever thought it could be."

"If this one works, he'll still need the other ear done at some point in time."

She nodded. "I'm trying not to forget that. Right now, though, I think I just need to get through this one."

"I can understand that. I just want you to keep it in the back of your mind that this is not the end of the line as far as surgery goes."

"Okay. How long do you think it'll be before I can see him?"

"A half hour. Maybe less."

She looked up at him. "I know you're

busy, but can you sit with me. Just for a few minutes while I absorb the news I so desperately needed?"

The news about Brody. Not about Wade. "Of course."

He dropped into the chair next to hers and pressed his shoulder against hers in a show of solidarity. She pulled in a deep breath and closed her eyes before slowly letting the air escape from her lungs. She repeated it again.

"God, it feels good just to breathe, doesn't it. We take it for granted, but we shouldn't."

Wade McKinna released from jail.

The suspicions that had appeared out of nowhere returned with a vengeance. The possibility was too horrible to imagine. It had to be for some petty crime or something more like tax evasion. There were myriad reasons why Lyndsey's ex-husband had spent time in prison. Except only one of them made sense to him right now.

But he wasn't going to ask her now. Not with her son lying in a hospital bed hoping beyond hope that he'd be able to hear again.

Unable to force his head to concentrate on anything beyond what Wade might or might not have done, Misha asked if she was ready to go see Brody.

"Absolutely. Do you think he's in a room yet?"

"If he's not, he soon will be, so let's head that way, and I'll tell you what to expect after his procedure."

It took ten minutes of explaining in minute detail what to look for over the next several days. But none of it was overly scary. It was pretty standard medical jargon.

By the time he finished, they'd reached the nurses' station. "Has Brody McKinna been put in a room yet?"

The nurse looked at a chart on her computer screen. "He's just being moved in." She smiled at Lyndsey. "He's evidently been asking for you repeatedly. Enough that it made it into the chart."

"Which room?" he asked.

"321. I would say wait until he's settled, but I know what it feels like to need to see your child after surgery. So go on in."

When Misha made a move to stay where

he was, Lyndsey sent him a glance. "Would you come with me? Please?"

With his heart in his throat, he nodded. Not because he'd never gone into a room to see a patient before, but because there was such a look of vulnerability in her eyes as she asked. There was no way he could refuse to go into that room with her.

Steeling himself to see her reaction, he went down the hall with her and pushed open the door to room 321.

Lyndsey had never seen a more beautiful sight than Brody lying in bed asleep. His long lashes cast shadows on his cheek, and his right ear had a pad of gauze placed over it.

She moved closer and touched his face, fingers feathering over her child's skin like she'd done when he'd been a little boy.

But he wasn't little anymore. He was on the cusp of being a man. Just a little younger than she and Misha had been when they'd first started dating.

It was enough to make her weep, but she forced herself to hold it together. It was one of the reasons she'd asked Misha to come in with her. The last thing she wanted to do was fall apart and drape herself over Brody's bed. He would hate that. He was a pretty stoic kid, and stoicism was what he reacted best to. A quiet, measured approach. He was so different from his dad, yet every once in a while she saw an expression that she recognized. It had bothered her at first, but she'd made her peace with it, reassuring herself that just because he might look like his father, it didn't mean Brody *was* his father. He was the polar opposite of him, in fact.

Brody's eyelids flickered and then slowly parted, his glassy eyes coming to rest on her, and then searching the room. She reached for his hand and gave it a squeeze. "You're okay. The surgery is all done." His gaze tracked back to her again before veering off. He said something nonsensical.

"Don't try to talk right now. Just rest for a while," she murmured. She was hyper aware of Misha standing just behind her not saying anything.

Brody shook his head. "I wish…" His

eyes rolled back for a second before coming back to rest on her. "I... I..."

The struggle to find the words broke her heart. Just as she was going to tell him again to rest, his free hand came up, fingers dangling, and kind of waved in Misha's direction.

"I..." Brody licked his lips and took a deep breath. "I wish you...you were my dad. Not...not Wade."

The room went silent, and Lyndsey's hand went to her mouth. She turned to look behind her, whispering the word "sorry" when she saw a muscle ticking away in his jaw.

Of all the things for Brody to say. He wasn't totally aware yet, but to think those words had been rolling around in his subconscious killed her. Because she had to admit she'd thought the same thing. Not because she was still in love with him, but because Misha would have made a great father. And because she wouldn't have had to do this all on her own.

She turned back toward the bed, suddenly exhausted. More exhausted than she could imagine.

When she felt something touch her shoulder, she flinched before she felt Misha give it a squeeze.

Brody was still looking at something behind her. At Misha?

When his big, reassuring voice came from behind her, she tensed. "If I were your dad, Brody, I wouldn't have been able to do your surgery."

"Oh, yeah. That would…have been bad. Very bad." Her son's gaze returned to her, and she could see the awareness trickling back in. He shook his head. "I don't know why I said that. I'm sorry, Mom."

She didn't think her heart could be more shattered than it was right now. "It's okay, baby. You're still waking up. People say silly things when they're under the effects of anesthesia."

Only this hadn't been something silly. Something she could easily laugh at and film for a later date. This was something that had come up from the depths of her son's soul. She had no idea he'd missed having a father that badly. And to choose someone he barely knew...

Well, Misha had probably attained hero status in his book. He'd repaired an ear that another doctor had said was beyond his scope of expertise. And he'd shown an interest in Brody's band and life. Maybe it was time to start limiting contact with Misha. No more side trips or invitations to events that were important to her son. The last thing she wanted was for him to be disappointed when Misha made it clear he had no interest in stepping in or filling any gaps that Brody might feel were there.

A snoring sound from the bed told her that he'd fallen back asleep. Thank God. Maybe next time he woke up, his head would be clearer. As it was, the idea of facing or talking to Misha was a horrifying specter that she couldn't banish.

She realized Misha's hand was still on her shoulder. A warm presence that she was reluctant to shake off. "I really am sorry. I can't believe he said that."

"It's perfectly okay. He'll probably be out for a couple of hours. Let's let him rest. I'm going to take a guess that you haven't eaten much this morning, since Brody wasn't allowed to have anything."

"I had some coffee." Which was now sitting in her stomach like an inky pool of acid.

"Let's go downstairs and grab a bite to eat."

"You don't have to babysit me. I am fine. And I'm sure you have other patients to see."

He shook his head. "Actually, not until tomorrow. Brody's surgery was complicated, and I wanted to make sure everything went okay, so he was the only thing I scheduled for today."

"Thanks so much. For everything." Okay, he was kind of gaining superhero status in her eyes as well, and she needed to be careful not to confuse gratitude with any more personal emotions.

Like wishing he really had been Brody's dad?

But he wasn't, and Brody wouldn't be Brody if he had been.

They reached the cafeteria, and they

went through the line. She picked up a couple of light choices, while Misha went for bacon and eggs. Her brows went up. "Did you not eat either?"

"I did, but nothing too heavy." He smiled. "This is how I celebrate a good outcome. And I can't imagine one better than Brody's."

"I can't believe it's finally done."

"Believe it. As long as his body adapts to the prosthesis, things should be fine." He pushed open the door to the courtyard and waited for her to go through first. It seemed like forever since the first time they met out there. But in reality, it was only a few weeks ago. He hadn't been happy to see her that day in his office, and she couldn't blame him.

And now? Was he over that initial shock?

He certainly seemed to be. And he hadn't reacted angrily to Brody's groggy pronouncement.

"I really am sorry for what happened in that room."

"He probably won't even remember saying it. Anesthesia meds suppress the centers that form lasting memories."

"I hope that's the case. He would be so mortified at having said what he did."

"Like I said, he more than likely won't remember anything about waking up. But I do want to ask you something regarding what Brody said."

He turned to look at her, his frown deep and ominous enough to make her shiver. "What did you want to ask?"

"I want to know what the hell that man did to you. And to Brody."

CHAPTER SEVEN

THERE WAS SILENCE for a few seconds, while she stared at him, eyes wide. "What do you mean?"

"I mean, I was coming to tell you about Brody's surgery and caught sight of the screen on Brittany's phone. I couldn't help but see the headline. Does his jail time have anything to do with you?"

She didn't speak for a full minute, and he thought maybe she was going to jump up, tell him to mind his own *proklyatiye* business and walk away. If she did, he wasn't going to stop her. But Brody's words had crunched something in his gut and the flash of anger it had brought with it was dangerous. If Wade had been in that room, he couldn't guarantee what he would have done to the man if what he thought was true really did turn out to be the case.

"Yes. It had to do with me."

"So I'm going to ask again. What did he do? And are you in any danger now?"

"There was a restraining order in place at the time of his arrest, so I'm hoping it's still in effect. I'll check with the courts before Brody and I return to the house."

He shut his eyes and counted to ten in Russian before looking at her again. "So he did hurt you. Your reaction to Joanna's injuries weren't just a fluke."

She shook her head. "No. It wasn't. She was pregnant. Just like I was at the time."

"*Der'mo…*" He couldn't stop the oath from escaping his mouth as he dragged his hand through his hair. Then he swiveled his body on the concrete bench, straddling it so he could face her fully. "Tell me." He said the words, even though he wasn't sure he wanted to hear what had transpired between her and her ex.

Lyndsey moistened her lips and then started talking, the words pouring out of her so quickly that he had to really concentrate to understand.

"When you left, Wade came and offered a shoulder to cry on. He listened. And he seemed like a perfect gentleman. And when he kissed me…." She shook her head. "I was so angry and confused, it was like everything inside of me rose up, and I accepted it. Maybe I was trying to get back at you, although I can see now how stupid that was.

"And when the kissing turned to other things, I never thought about protection. My emotions were just too dark…too raw."

"You got pregnant." A dark pit of anger and despair opened up inside of him, threatening to swallow him whole. But he had to know. Had to understand the ramifications his decision to leave had had on Lyndsey.

"Yes. And he offered marriage immediately."

She'd obviously accepted. And looking at it through her eyes, he could see how that might have seemed like the best solution for everyone.

She appeared to gather herself together. "What I didn't know at the time was that he was secretly taking steroids to improve his ball playing. There were scouts looking to fill their college rosters, and Wade was determined to get on one of them. But as the months rolled by, the offers dried up. Maybe Wade's attitude had turned them off. I'm not sure. What I do know is that he started getting angry, and I was the only one around."

He suddenly knew he didn't want to hear the rest of it, but he'd asked the question, and Lyndsey obviously needed to talk to someone about it.

"It started off as ridicule. I didn't dress the right way or talk the right way. He became convinced that the colleges saw his marital status as a detriment. According to him, they wanted single quarterbacks that the girls would flock around. And by that time I was six months pregnant and felt huge and ungainly. Wade started drilling into my head that I was the reason he wasn't getting any offers. And I found myself starting to believe him. When we were out in public, I shrank back and tried my best to become invisible."

"Ethot ubludoc." More words slipped out before he could stop them. But they were true. Wade was a bastard. Cowardly and cruel.

"I don't know what that means."

"You don't want to know. I take it Wade's abuse didn't begin and end with words. It escalated?"

"He tried to blame it on 'roid rage, but there were other girls with similar stories. Some of them during the time we were married. When no scholarships appeared, he started drinking, making what was already a bad situation even worse. He hit me for the first time a week later. He was so remorseful afterwards, and looking back, I can't believe I fell for his promises that it would never happen again.

"Worse, Brittany came and told me that he'd hit on her when he saw her at the store." She pulled in a deep breath. "That night he came home drunk. And when I wouldn't go to bed with him and confronted him about what Brittany had said, he grabbed me, put his hands around my throat…"

"God, Lynds."

"I thought I was going to die. And if it hadn't been for the thought of Brody, I might have. I clawed at his hands with all my might and kneed him in the groin, and he let go. And then I ran and ran and ran, until a neighbor took me into her house and called the police." She bit her lip. "He was sentenced to fifteen years in prison for attempted murder. And that's what you saw on Brittany's phone. He just got out."

"No wonder she hates me so much." He said the words more to himself than anything.

Lyndsey looked at him for a long time, before reaching out and touching his hand. "Brittany doesn't hate you. She hates what happened. And it wasn't your fault. None of it. I made those choices. Not you."

"But if I hadn't left…"

She needed to speak the truth, even if the circumstances around it still hurt. "If you hadn't left, I wouldn't have Brody. It's as simple and as complicated as that."

"Even so. What Wade did—"

"That's on Wade. Not anyone else. And I wouldn't trade my son for anything. Like I said, he saved my life. Literally. And my mom worships the ground he walks on. She loves him. Does it excuse anything Wade did? Absolutely not. And I should have left sooner. But it was hard reconciling the charming star quarterback that I thought I knew with the monster he could become."

"Has he tried to contact you?"

"Yes. And he's begged me to bring Brody to see him at the prison." She touched his hand again. "Brody doesn't know exactly what happened between me and his dad. I haven't told him. I just told him that he went to prison for doing some very bad stuff. And Brody has never once asked to see him. And maybe he knows more. The news articles are out there. And I'm sure some of his friends probably heard about it from their parents. But if he has, he's never said anything."

Brody was a smart kid. And curious. Like Lynds said, he probably knew more than she thought, which may be where his anesthesia-induced comments came from.

"I want to take you home tonight, once Brody is discharged. Stay the night. Make sure everything is okay at your house."

"I'm sure Wade wouldn't—"

"Maybe not. But I could see someone like him wanting to take some swipes at you. Even though he did all of this to himself. I don't trust him. I never have."

She squirmed. "My car is still in the shop, which is why Brittany was here with me. I planned on staying the night at a hotel."

"Please, Lyndsey. I would never forgive myself if something happened to you or Brody."

She looked down at her food, then back up at him. "I'll accept, but only because of Brody. If there's any hint of him trying to come near us, I'll call the police."

"I can sleep on the couch."

"No need. We have a spare bedroom that my parents use from time to time when I've had to go out of town. And no, it's not the house Wade and I shared. That was in his name, and he sold it off to pay for his defense."

"Defense. That's kind of laughable when you think about it. There's no defending what he did."

"No. Like I said, he tried to blame it on the steroids, but they were able to prove that there was already a pattern of behavior that began in high school. It just wasn't common knowledge. The drugs amplified what was already present. My hope is that he'll leave the area and Brody and I will never have to deal with him again. His parents both passed while he was in prison so there's nothing really holding him here."

The anger that had been flickering in the background flared up. "If he's smart, that's exactly what he'll do. But in case he doesn't, I want to be there for a night or two."

"One night." She smiled. "I'm really a pretty self-sufficient person nowadays."

"Of that I have no doubt."

She glanced down at her plate. "Wow, I can't believe I actually ate it all. I must have been hungrier than I thought."

His fingers moved to hers and linked with them for a few seconds before giving them a quick squeeze and then releasing them, despite the fact that he hadn't quite been ready to let her go. "Thank you for telling me. And for letting me take you home."

In a different place and time that last sentence would have had an entirely different connotation. But it wasn't. It was here and now, and he had no right to expect anything to change between them. His mom had called him last night to let him know he had a new baby cousin. She'd been disappointed that he wouldn't come home to welcome the newborn into the family. But Louisiana was his home now. If his mom became ill, he would of course go and take care of her, but he couldn't see himself staying there for the long term. When he settled down—if he settled down—he wanted it to be here. Wanted to raise any children he might have here.

Not that there were any prospects. He had no interest in trying to meet people. So maybe he would someday die here, alone with no family to stand beside him.

Something that was ridiculous to think about right now.

"I appreciate your concern, Misha, although I'm pretty sure Wade isn't stupid enough to try anything. I'll call Brittany and let her know you'll be driving me home and staying the night."

"I'm sure she'll be over the moon when she hears that news."

"She'll be glad that I'm safe. Like I said, her problem isn't with you. Well, not most of it, anyway."

One brow went up. "That's so very reassuring, Lynds."

She laughed. "She's overprotective, and I love her. I'd do the same for her."

"Speaking of overprotective, how about we go and check in on Brody, while I get the ball rolling on his discharge papers."

"I can't believe you're releasing him already."

"He's fine. He's going to be in pain until some of the swelling goes down, but pain meds should help take care of that. Unfortunately, I'd rather not use any of my so-called magic drops in his ear, due to the risk of them getting into the surgical site. And seriously. Is there really an elf in a drawer at the nurses' station?"

"There really is. And his name really is Ornery. He's an expert in dealing with difficult patients that happen to be under the age of ten or so."

"That is crazy. And yet it obviously works."

"It does indeed." She tilted her head as she looked at him. "Speaking of kids. What if Brody remembers what he said earlier? How should we handle that?"

The "we" in that sentence gave him a wobbly feeling that he couldn't quite banish. It would be easy to get used to that. To making joint decisions with someone about a child.

Hadn't he just thought about having a family someday?

But Brody wasn't his, and Lyndsey hadn't meant it the way he'd taken it. She wasn't likely to ask him for parenting advice.

"I think we laugh it off. I'll say something off the wall and funny. I'm good at that."

"Really? The person who can't tell a joke to save his life?"

He cocked a brow. "I did have my moments, if you remember right."

"Yes, you did. Just not in the stand-up comedy department." When she gave him that cheeky smile from the past, he knew what she was thinking of. The times they'd made love until neither of them could see straight. And afterward, more often than not, they'd start the process all over again.

"Careful, Lynds. You might wind up with more than you bargained for."

"Sorry." It was as if she pulled herself together in a rush, suddenly remembering where she was, who she was with. If he wasn't careful, she was going to change her mind about letting him drive her home, and right now, her and Brody's safety trumped everything. He forced himself to look at that goal and nothing more.

"Let's go see him."

With that, they dumped their trash and

walked to the elevators that would take them up to the third floor.

This time, Brody was definitely awake and in his right mind. And as Misha had suspected, he didn't mention anything about Wade or wishing that Misha was his dad. He was fingering the dressing over his ear. "How long does this have to stay on? My ear feels full."

His voice was a little raspy from being intubated, but other than that he wasn't complaining of pain. That would come later.

"That's normal. And the dressing has to stay on a couple of days. We don't want any dirt or dust introduced to your ear until your bone has a chance to heal."

"Where you drilled the hole?"

"Yes."

"And my music?"

"That's a harder answer, but it's necessary, Brody. You need to reintroduce certain sounds slowly. Nothing loud or full of bass for a couple of weeks. We want to see how the prosthesis handles everything. And like I said, I want it to have a chance to heal before it does any heavy lifting."

The boy blew out a breath. "I know you mentioned all of this before, but now that I've had the surgery, everything seems very real. Is it really going to work? I feel like I can't hear anything out of that ear right now and it's freaking me out a little bit."

"I know. But like I said, you need to heal. There's some swelling from where I had to drill, I'm sure. That will take a few days to subside. Then we'll bring you in for some hearing tests and see where we stand."

"And if it works, I'll have to go through it all over again with my left ear?"

"Yes." He didn't want to give false hope that things might stabilize. Otosclerosis was progressive and there was evidence that his left ear was already being affected, although not nearly as much as his right ear had been. But it would get there. It was better for Brody to be prepared for that eventuality. "But you'll be surprised at how quickly this will go."

Lyndsey moved to the head of the bed. "Let's just take this one ear at a time, okay? No jumping ahead to a place we can't yet see."

"Okay." And with that, the conversation about the surgery took a back seat as his mom handed Brody his phone and let him check his messages.

He smiled. "Most of my friends have texted me." His eyes widened. "And one of my bandmates said he's writing a song that he wants me to sing. About my hearing. Listen to the chorus.'

As I sit here in my silence, wondering what is next,
The fear is overwhelming. Is there really nothing left?
Then a tiny blip of sound bursts through my brokenness.
Just a hint of treble. Followed by a touch of bass.
Is any of this possible?
Can a miracle break through?
Or is it all a wishful dream that never will come true?

"Oh, Brody. That is beautiful. I…" She shook her head as if unable to finish her thought. Instead, she leaned over and hugged him for a long moment.

She wasn't the only one who'd been touched by those words. Misha's insides were twisted with emotion. This could have been referring to his first weeks in Belarus after leaving Lyndsey behind. As his dad battled his cancer.

When he could finally bring himself to speak, he said, "That is a keeper, Brody."

"It's awesome. He knows I can't play right now, but they still want to get together and figure out the rest of the lyrics and the music. Maybe use this time to write some original stuff."

Who said high school students weren't wise? He was certainly seeing a whole lot of wisdom in this particular group.

"That's wonderful," Lyndsey said. "Blessings we can't always see at first, but they're in there, waiting on their chance to peek through all the bad stuff."

Was she talking about her marriage to Wade? About Brody's hearing? Maybe a little bit of both.

Brody nodded. "When can I go home? I want to get started on this."

There was an unmistakable excitement in his voice. The same giddy happiness that he'd had when describing the music festival. His passion and thirst for it were unmistakable. Who knew if he would someday make it in the music industry. He certainly seemed to have the drive for it.

"Let me check you over really quickly and then we can see about breaking you out of here."

Misha was smart enough to realize the next surgery was going to be tricky, if he stayed this particular course. He wasn't related to either Lyndsey or Brody, but he was getting attached. He could feel those threads relentlessly tugging at him. At least when it came to Brody. Would he know when he'd crossed that line?

Or had he already crossed it? Maybe it was time to start researching other ENTs who had expertise in this field, although he was pretty sure Lyndsey would fight him on it. But it wasn't just about the attachments. It was about whether he could objectively do his job if a complication arose. Or would he freeze?

He had no idea, because he'd never been faced with this kind of dilemma before. And to admit to Lyndsey that he cared about Brody too much to continue to be his doctor?

He could imagine her face if he shared that kind of news. She'd be angry. Furious, probably. And he'd be railing over his inability to keep his thoughts and feelings to himself.

Going to her house to make sure it was safe? Did a doctor do that for the parents of his patients? Or just the ones he cared for a little too much?

Maybe a part of him wished that he was Brody's dad too.

But they were a ways out from his next stapedotomy. He still had time to slow down what was happening. But not today. Not when he needed to make sure Lyndsey and Brody were safe. If that wrote him out of the picture as far as being able to provide medical care for the boy, then so be it. He would cross that bridge when he came to it.

He did a quick exam, checking the covering on his ear for excess drainage or active bleeding. There was none. And his blood pressure and vitals were all within the normal range.

"All right. Let's get those discharge papers started."

Lyndsey stepped forward. "Misha will be coming home with us, just to make sure everything is okay overnight."

He wasn't sure he agreed with her about keeping the real reason from her son, but she hadn't technically lied.

"Cool! Will he be in Gram's room?"

Why would Brody think he'd be sleeping anywhere else? Had other men come over who hadn't stayed in that third bedroom?

Something he really didn't want to think about. And something that was none of his business. He'd slept with other women after their breakup. So why should it be any different for her. It wasn't. He was just being an ass.

"Yes, he will. And just for tonight."

He was pretty sure that last part carried

a message for him, that one night was all he was allowed.

They wheeled Brody out of the hospital in the required wheelchair, pulling up beside Misha's Jeep.

"Can we put the top down today?"

He smiled. "No. Not with your ear the way it is. Maybe another time."

As if there would be one.

Brody was able to get in the back under his own power and buckled himself in. "My ear is starting to throb a little."

"That's to be expected. We'll pick up your prescription on the way home." He glanced at Lyndsey, who rattled off the name of a pharmacy in Centerville. Then she twisted to look back at her son. "By the way, no talking on the phone tonight, young man."

"Mom! I'm not totally stupid. We text most of the time anyway. It's easier."

Misha smiled. He wasn't exactly sure how typing out messages on a tiny phone screen was faster than just saying the words into the phone, but maybe he was just a little slower when it came to technology.

Besides, he received more texts in a day than he cared to count. He was happy when his phone sat somewhere without pinging every few seconds.

When she looked over at him, he could have sworn she was thinking the exact same thing. In fact, she gave a choked sound that could have even been a laugh. He liked seeing her this way. It was like a huge weight had been lifted from her shoulders, which was odd since the reason he was spending the night at her house should have her just the slightest bit worried.

"Maybe I should have had the prescription called in here in Lafayette instead of Centerville."

"How bad is your ear, Brody?" he asked.

"It's okay. It's just hurting a little. I can make it home."

He paused. "Actually, can you move across to the left side of the car? I'd rather you didn't rest the right side of your head against the window." The vibrations might aggravate where the prosthesis is attached to the footplate of the old stapes.

He waited to start the car until Brody was buckled in behind him. If he fell asleep, he'd feel better about his head resting on the opposite side. Unfortunately, he didn't carry a pillow or a blanket in the car, because it was rare that he ever carried passengers in here. Actually, going to the music festival was one of the few times he could remember anyone besides him being in the vehicle, unless it was for a business lunch with colleagues, which didn't happen all that often either.

They pulled out onto the highway and headed in the direction of Centerville.

CHAPTER EIGHT

LYNDSEY WOKE UP with a start, feeling out of sorts as she tried to figure out where she was. Then she realized. Misha's car. It was no longer moving, and they were parked in her driveway. But there was no sign of either her son or Misha. And the vehicle's back door on the side where Brody was sitting was hanging wide open. The seat was empty.

A sense of horror set in. Had Wade been there waiting for them? Had he kidnapped Brody? Hurt or killed Misha?

Leaping out of the car, her legs barely held her upright as she struggled to run up the walk toward the front door, which was also wide open. It was like one of those movies where something held you glued to the ground, while everything around you moved in slow motion.

"Brody!" Her son's name came out as a long scream of pain.

Misha appeared just in time to catch her as she fell through the doorway. He held onto her as she flailed around, trying to break free.

"What the hell?" he said. "What's wrong?"

She stared at him, her mouth opening and closing several times. "Me? Where is Brody? Where *is* he?"

"He's in bed."

"In bed." She tried to wrap her head around what he'd just said. "So Wade didn't…he's not…?"

"*O milyy*... No, no, no." He gathered her tightly in his arms. "I'm so sorry. I carried Brody into the house. You were both fast asleep and I didn't want to disturb either of you. I never dreamed you might wake up and think…"

She clung to him as relief caused her limbs to buckle, her racing heart making her dizzy. "I've only been that scared one time in my whole life."

He dropped a soft kiss onto her temple. "I'm sorry." He crooned something over and over in his native tongue. She wasn't sure what it was, but she could feel her heartbeat slow, his calm, even voice soothing her nerves in a way she'd never known.

Brody was okay. Misha had somehow wrestled him into the house, although her son was almost as tall as she was.

She was suddenly glad Misha was here. The thought of walking into that empty house and wondering if someone was waiting there inside…

A thought occurred. "How did you get in?"

This time he looked a bit chagrined. "Your keys were hanging from the shoulder strap of your purse so I…took them."

She nodded. "Thank you. Thank you so much."

"I'm not sure if you should be thanking me or cursing me. I never meant to scare you."

"I jumped to conclusions and wasn't thinking straight." She glanced up at him.

"Okay, I think I can stand up on my own now."

He let her go gingerly, as if he wasn't as sure as she was that she could manage it. "Do you think any of your neighbors called the police on us?"

Oh, God. That was the last thing she needed. "You mean because of my banshee-like shriek?"

"I wasn't going to say it, but it certainly had me skidding my way to the door." He gave her a half grin that made her insides turn to mush.

"I'll text the ones I know and tell them everything's fine." She retrieved her phone from her pocketbook, surprised it was still on her arm with the way she'd leapt out of the car. Pressing a few keys, she reassured the neighbors she knew that all was well.

"I'll go out and close up and lock the car."

She glanced back and saw that not only Brody's car door was still open, but hers was too. "You must think I'm absolutely insane."

"No. I think you're a mother who loves her child."

"Thanks."

"Let me make you a cup of coffee. I see you have one that uses the pods. I think I can figure that kind out. Cream? Sugar?"

"Thank you. Both. I have flavored creamer in the fridge. I'm going to check on Brody."

"You go. He's got his pain meds on board, I hope you don't mind. He woke up long enough to take it. Right before I heard you scream."

She managed a low laugh. "You are never going to let me live that down, are you?"

"*Net.*"

Even she knew what that word meant. "Gee, thanks."

She headed toward Brody's room and when she got there, true to Misha's word, her son was fast asleep. His shoes were tucked under the bed and his covers were tucked around his narrow form. He looked peaceful and vulnerable. She knelt on the floor beside his bed and stared at him. She didn't know what she'd do if something ever happened to him.

But it hadn't. She leaned her cheek on the mattress next to him and breathed out a prayer of thanks. First thing tomorrow she was going to check on that restraining order and whether or not the prison knew where Wade was headed. Surely, he was on parole and had to report things like that. Not that any of it was a guarantee that he wouldn't try to contact her or Brody. Maybe it was time to tell her son the truth and make sure he knew how dangerous it was to have anything to do with his dad.

When she finally got up and walked back to the living room, she spied two coffee cups on the glass-topped coffee table in front of the couch. A wash of gratitude went through her, not just for the coffee, but for taking at least one layer of worry off her. Brittany had already texted her a few times since they left the hospital, and she'd finally been able to reassure her friend that she was fine and would let her know if she could do anything.

"Thank you." She sat on the leather couch, letting the soft cushions envelope her.

He handed her a cup and she wrapped her hands around it, letting the warmth seep into the iciness of her hands. She didn't even want to think about the shape she'd be in if her worst fears had come to life—if they'd pulled up to her driveway and found Wade waiting for her.

When Misha sat next to her and put his arm around her, she leaned into him, breathing deep and taking a sip of her coffee. She allowed herself to fully relax. Oh, how she'd missed this closeness. Missed the sight and scent of him. Missed how perfectly she fit against his side, her cheek nestled against the warmth of his neck.

It had been even better on hot nights when his shirt had come over his head and she'd been able to snuggle against his bare skin. And the times when it wasn't only his shirt that had come off…

Oh, yes. Those had been the best times. But for now, she was happy to just cruise down memory lane and enjoy this tiny taste of the past.

Neither of them said anything as they drank their coffees. The silence was both wonderful and healing. A balm to her soul.

She thought of the first line in Brody's song. *As I sit here in my silence...*

Silence could mean so many things. It could mean physical silence. Anguish. Grief. Or it could mean comfort and peace, which was what it meant for her right now.

"This is nice."

"Yes, it is, *milyy.*" His voice rumbled over her. Through her. All around her. The familiar endearment pulling at her insides.

She couldn't stop herself from tilting her head and looking up at him. The blue eyes gazing back at her contained a crystalline warmth that made her want to stroke tiny circles over the pressure points in his temples until his eyelids swept closed in pleasure.

He was so gorgeous. And he'd once been hers. How had that even happened?

Before she could stop herself, she rolled

her body until her front faced his and her thighs were on either side of his.

His face tightened. "Lynds…"

"Tell me you don't feel it." She couldn't help herself. After all that had happened today, she just needed to touch him. Needed to be touched by him.

Wrapping one arm around her back to secure her to him, he leaned forward to put his coffee cup on the table in front of them. "Oh, I feel it. But if you're planning to end this before it gets fully started, I suggest you move to a different location."

She moistened her lips, wondering if she dared. Yes. She did.

Her hands went to his shoulders and her hips slid forward until she was pressed tight against him. And yes, she definitely felt something there. "You mean like…this location?"

He groaned. "Lyndsey, I'm not playing around."

She cupped his face, her thumbs sliding over his cheeks, his eyelids, anything she could reach. "Does it feel like I'm playing?"

"No. It feels like you're about to get exactly what you're asking for. If you are asking, that is."

"Oh, I am. I definitely am."

He glanced at the closed door across the room. "What if Brody comes out and sees us?"

True. She hadn't quite thought about that. "This is kind of a compromising position, isn't it? My bedroom is just down that hallway," she whispered. "As far from his as we can get."

Without hesitation he stood, his arms going beneath her butt to carry her along with him. He then strode to the door and pushed it open, turning and pushing it quietly shut again with his foot. Then he locked it. "It looks like I won't be using your spare bedroom after all." He smiled at her before moving to the bed and unceremoniously dropping her onto the mattress. She squeaked at the unexpectedness of it.

"No, it looks like you won't."

There was no fear in her as he undressed her with slow, careful hands before turning to his own clothing. No fear. Only the pleasure of getting to look at him again, when fifteen years ago, she was sure she'd never have that chance again. Never get to feel his touch again.

And yet here he was. The terrain of his body had changed slightly, but it was still familiar in ways that beckoned to her. Her body had changed as well. And yet, he obviously still desired her. Because he was here. In her house. In her bedroom.

But for how long?

The insidious whisper slithered through her, winding around her synapses and halting the steady flow of communication between her brain and her body.

No. She wasn't going to let anything ruin this. She was going to enjoy this night for what it was: the gift of one more time, when she'd thought there was none to be had.

His palms glided up her thighs, making her squirm with need. "You'll tell me if you don't like something, *milyy*?"

Was that a reference to Wade and what she'd told him? Misha would never do anything to purposely hurt her.

"I like it all."

He sighed, the sound sliding over her like a caress. "Do you…like this?" His palms came to a halt just below her hip bones, his thumbs grazing over the v at the tops of her thighs.

Her breath whooshed in at the jolt of sensation. So close. And yet not close enough.

"Yes. I like it."

He lingered only for a second or two before continuing his journey up her body, dancing over her ribcage with soft swipes of his hands. "And this?"

He had to know he was driving her crazy. Her gaze ran over his body, eyes moving down to the obvious need that was very much on display. She wanted that with a desperation that made her whimper. "Yes." She beckoned to him with her hands. "Misha, come here."

"My pleasure." He lowered himself onto the bed, fitting his hips in the juncture of her thighs. "And now, I can do this…"

His mouth moved over her left breast with tiny kisses that pebbled her nipples and made her arch into him. "Yes."

And then he was there, sucking her into

his mouth, sending fiery shots of need racing through her. She twined her legs around his, desperately seeking a friction that he hadn't given her yet. Looping her arms around his neck, she pulled him in for her kiss, her tongue sliding deep into his mouth.

His groaned response told her all she needed to know. He used to love this when they were together. And he evidently still loved it. That knowledge was satisfying in a way she didn't quite understand. And maybe she didn't want to. But it made her feel powerful. And in control. It was heady. And awe-inspiring.

His hands went to either side of her face, caressing her cheeks, her lips, his fingertips periodically touching her tongue as it continued to press forward in his mouth in a way that was so very sensuous.

Everything about this man was built for sex. His physique. His hands…his voice. That voice that could send shivers down her spine with a single syllable. It was rough and throaty, the Russian intonations scraping across her senses like callused hands on her most sensitive spots.

He did it for her. He always had. From the moment she'd met him all those years ago.

He still did.

She didn't fear Misha. But she feared that. The craving for him that hadn't lessened after all these years.

It was okay. She was giving herself permission to crave him. But just for tonight. So she had to make it worth both their whiles. She untwined her legs. Loosened her arms from around his neck. Pulled free from his mouth.

When he lifted his head to look at her, a frown darkened his face. She smiled. "Don't worry. This isn't the end. It's just the beginning."

With that, she pushed hard at his chest, rolling him onto his back. Before he could do anything, she had straddled him, just like she'd done on the couch. She pressed her hands onto the mattress on either side of his head, leaning over him, her hair falling around them.

"It's your turn to tell me what you like. Do you like this?" She slid her tongue across his lips, darting inside for a second then sliding back out.

"You know I do."

"I do know." She leaned down and kissed him softly. Slowly. "But pretend that I don't."

She moved her hips forward, sliding over his erection with slow steady pressure that made him jerk against her.

His hands moved to her hips, holding them still as if his life depended on it.

"I liked that a little too much."

"Did you?" She licked her lips. "Then show me."

She took one of his hands and drew it to his flesh, wrapping his fingers around it and holding it there with her own. "Show me, Misha."

His eyes on hers, he slowly pumped his hand, a muscle ticking in his jaw as if trying to keep a tight hold on his control. Seeing him this way pushed her own need to an all-time high. Less than a minute later, he let go and lifted her up and onto him, seating her all the way down in one quick move.

"Ahh…" her breath whistled through

suddenly tight vocal cords, the numbing pleasure almost overtaking her. If he had moved another inch, she would have gone over the edge. But he didn't. He held her there. Tight against him.

They stayed completely still, and she saw the strain in his beautiful face as he wrestled to hold back.

Suddenly she didn't want to hold back. Didn't want to wait. Maybe there would be other times, and yet here they were acting as if they were going to fall off the face of the earth if they let themselves go.

She looked at him. Really looked at him.

"Misha. It's okay."

He understood exactly what she was saying, his body relaxing as he allowed himself to feel. As he allowed *her* to feel.

And it was an ecstasy of a different kind as they relearned their rhythm. The one that had once been so natural, so unique to them as a couple. He knew just how much pressure to put where. Knew that rotating his pubic bone against that tiny nub of flesh could drive her wild with need. And so he did, with each thrust of his hips.

And it was good and familiar and...*them*.

Lyndsey let it flow around her, the snapping electricity that crackled and coaxed and periodically bit.

She let herself rise and fall in tune with his body's moves, the realization that she had never felt so in sync with another human being as she had with Misha.

Pleasure washed over her, the waves rushing in and then flowing out, making her anticipate when they would come again. Her hands wouldn't be still, needing to touch him everywhere. He was the same, and God, she wasn't sure she would ever be whole again by the time they were done.

Misha's thumb touched her, and the shock of the direct contact made her go still, her every nerve ending focusing inward on that pleasure center. He teased and coaxed and demanded. Her hips made a shuddery descent and then rose again before pushing back down with an urgency that swelled inside of her.

"Yes, *milyy,* just like that."

She kept going, her rhythm quickening to match his thumb's movements. The fingers of his free hand intertwined with hers, creating an intimacy that drove her even higher.

She couldn't hold back anymore. Didn't want to hold back. She suddenly pumped with jerky movements, her control slipping from her fingers. And then it was here, the wave that crashed over her...pulsed around her, giving everything up. She moaned, leaning over and taking his mouth, kissing him like there was no tomorrow.

No tomorrow.

She closed her eyes as the world began to slow and her movements with it. She felt, more than saw, Misha carry their joined hands to his mouth and kiss them And something about that gesture...

No tomorrow.

It finally entered her brain, bringing with it the reality that the thought probably held an element of truth.

Hadn't she thought how good it was to have him one more time?

And now she had. It was already in the past. As if defying that reality, her hips rose one last time before settling with a finality against him.

She wanted to cry. But she wasn't going to.

Gentle fingers touched her cheek, and she realized one tear had already escaped somehow.

"Lynds…are you okay?"

She forced a smile and somehow manufactured a satisfied sigh. "Yes. You?"

Twining his fingers in her hair, he drew her down for a kiss. "More than okay. That was…*potryasayushchiy*."

She had no idea what that word meant. She only knew it was good. Very good.

"So are you, Misha."

And now it was time. Time to move back to reality. Before she could chicken out, she lifted her hips, allowing him to slide free. Each second she stayed joined to him was another second that she wanted to ask him to stay. In more ways than one. But she couldn't. At least not yet.

"*Net*." His soft complaint caught at her soul.

"We have to. Brody is just down the hallway."

It had nothing to do with Brody, and everything to do with self-preservation, but it was the only excuse she could think of.

He tugged her onto the bed and moved in close behind her, wrapping his arm around her. "Then let me lie with you for a while. I promise I'll be in the other bedroom by morning."

How could she argue with that, when she wanted so badly to feel him against her, to imagine them as they were all those years ago. Hadn't he said the same thing to her then, as they lay together in her bedroom?

"Let me lie with you for a while. I promise I'll be gone by morning."

And Misha had always kept that promise. Sometime in the middle of the night, as she slept, he would silently slip from her bed. In the morning, she was always alone.

As those words filtered through her, a part of her mourned. Because in the morning…tomorrow morning. She would be all alone.

Just as she always was.

CHAPTER NINE

MISHA HADN'T GONE to the spare bedroom. In the early hours of dawn, he had lain in Lyndsey's bed and watched her sleep for a long time, already knowing he wasn't going to press her for anything more than what they'd shared last night.

She'd tossed and turned, one time crying out the word "no!" in her sleep. It had ripped through him in a way that had him gritting his teeth in pain. Was her restlessness due to what they'd shared? She'd said she liked it, but maybe something inside said something else. Or maybe it was memories of Wade. Memories that sleeping with Misha had reawakened? Either way, her sleep was not that of someone who was at ease with where they were. With who they were with.

Why couldn't things ever be simple for them?

He had no idea. But they weren't. And for the life of him, he couldn't figure out a way to magically make them so.

The reality was Lyndsey had a teenaged son who might lose his hearing in his left ear if he didn't have surgery. A surgery Misha was no longer sure he could perform.

And if nothing else he'd ever done had hurt her, refusing to operate on Brody would. And he wasn't sure he knew how to tell her.

Unless he could somehow turn this ship around and put them back on solidly professional ground. That meant not seeing her. Not touching her. Not going to anything special that Brody might want him to go to.

But there was one thing he could never unhear, and it was Brody saying, *I wish you were my dad and not Wade.*

He wasn't sure how he would get past that statement enough to be objective. Because in his heart of hearts, last night as he'd lain in that bed and watched a sleeping Lyndsey, he'd wished the very same thing, that it had been him who'd made a family with her and not Wade.

So he'd slipped from her bed in the early morning hours and quietly exited the house, locking the front door and pulling it tight. Then he'd gone out to his car and sat in it and watched to make sure no one tried to creep in while Lyndsey and Brody were asleep. When the sun came up and neighbors started stirring, he knew it was safe to leave. So he drove to his office before anyone got there and sat at his desk. He then laid his head on the flat surface and set his watch alarm before letting himself get a couple of hours rest. Maybe by then, the answer would come to him.

The awkwardness was the worst. She knew he was trying hard to maintain a professional demeanor in front of their colleagues, but it was slowly driving her crazy. She'd woken up three days ago—after making crazy love to him—to an empty house. Oh, Brody was there. And she'd thought

Misha was too. So she'd cooked this fabulous breakfast, thinking that maybe she'd overreacted the night before. Surely, they didn't have to go back to being strangers.

But when she'd sent Brody to wake Misha up, his son came back with a frown. "He's not there." He shook his head. "It doesn't look like he even slept in the bed."

She'd gone to see for herself. He was right. There'd been no sign of Misha having been in that room. Had she imagined the whole thing? She moved the wrong way and a twinge in a certain region told her muscles that hadn't been used in years had indeed been put to the test during the night. And what a test it was. It had been everything she could have hoped for.

Then why had he left the way he had?

She hadn't asked him when she saw him the next day because he was acting funny. Kind of withdrawn. Like he didn't want to be seen talking to her. She'd backed off immediately and thought she'd try the next day. But he was the same way yesterday.

It was now a week after Brody's surgery, and today she didn't even try. She'd gone to the courthouse yesterday and found out that in his release agreement, Wade wasn't allowed to come anywhere near her or Brody. Nor was he allowed to contact them. That helped alleviate her fear a little bit. But it was still there humming in the background, and honestly, it might always be that way. A man that had once hurt her was out there somewhere, and the way Misha was acting, there was no way she was going to call him if she was afraid in the middle of the night.

Actually, Brody had a follow-up appointment with him at ten this morning and she didn't want to get into a big discussion about that night and somehow cause a bigger rift than there already was.

It was as if that night had never happened. Or maybe he only wished it had never happened.

God. She hoped he didn't present this strained, unfriendly side to her son too. It would hurt him. Maybe she should go talk to him before the appointment and ask him what was wrong.

But in the end, she chickened out. Besides, he was doing the exact thing that she'd originally planned to do: pull back and protect herself and Brody.

She hadn't needed to withdraw, because he'd done it for her. And actually, she wasn't thrilled with it.

And now it was ten, and Misha was late. Brody on the other hand was brimming with excitement at the idea of getting the packing and gauze removed from his ear. They would also be testing his hearing for the first time since the surgery.

Fifteen minutes later, Misha breezed into the room as if he didn't have a care in the world and sat behind the desk. "Hello, Brody, how are you feeling?"

He said nothing to her, and it stung more than it should have. But if he didn't want to interact with her, then that was his prerogative. Hell, she'd supposedly prepared herself for just this possibility. So why wasn't she handling it better than she was.

Brody looked from her to Misha with a frown. It was kind of hard *not* to notice the tension between them was thick enough to cut with a knife. And her kid was nothing if not intuitive.

But in the end, all that mattered was that Misha talk to Brody about his surgery and the possible outcomes. She was his mother, yes, but she was positive Misha wouldn't move in a direction that she wouldn't approve of. He wasn't that kind of man. Or that kind of doctor.

"I'm looking forward to getting this stuff out of my ear." He smiled at Misha.

There was no return smile. "You know you won't be able to submerge your head for three more weeks. I have some ear plugs you can use, if you go swimming. But it's very important until your eardrum fully heals. Do you understand?"

Brody's head tilted as he looked at the man. "Sure. I get it."

"And no heavy lifting for the same period of time."

Brody nodded, but his frown had grown, and she knew why. Because Misha had gone from acting like a friend to acting like a doctor who was seeing a routine patient.

Brody was hurt by the change. Just like she knew he would be.

And, oh, how she knew that hurt. She'd

felt it for the past week. Did he regret their night together so much that he'd had to withdraw into his little box and close the lid so that she and Brody had no access except that which he allowed? Which was pretty much none at all.

And it stunk. It stunk for Brody who'd had no say in what the two adults had done that night. And it stunk for her, who'd not fully weighed the possible ramifications of sleeping with him again.

How easy he made it seem to walk away. Whether it was emotionally, like he was doing right now, or physically like he'd done back in high school. She hadn't seen him after he'd left for Belarus, but she remembered thinking she hoped he was suffering as much as she was. But seeing him now? She doubted he had. There was some wall he was able to erect that kept him from looking at anything except what he chose to look at. And right now, that wall was keeping him from seeing them. Really, seeing them. It was as if he could talk to them without looking at them.

Doing it to her was one thing. But doing it to Brody?

Hell no. As soon as this appointment was over, she was going to have it out with him. He could damn well be late for his next appointment just like he'd been late for theirs, while she had her say.

"Why don't you hop up on that table, and we'll see what we've got." He finally gave her son a smile that didn't quite make it to his eyes.

By the time he'd silently removed layers of gauze and packing and examined Brody's ear with the otoscope, Lyndsey was boiling mad.

She could practically see Brody shrinking into himself as if he sensed Misha's indifference to him as a person. All Misha seemed interested in were the results of the procedure he'd done on him. Stoking his own ego?

No. She didn't think so. Misha had never been egotistical. So what was going on?

They went through a few hearing tests using the tuning fork again, as well as the booth where an audiologist measured his hearing.

Brody came out of the booth and the audiologist handed the results to Misha, who rested a hip on the exam table. Brody came over and sat next to her, no longer even trying to engage with him.

And Misha seemed oblivious to the change in his patient. "So, how do you feel the hearing in your right ear is? Better? Worse? No change?"

"It's better."

The words were said in a monotone that bothered her. He'd been so very excited about this appointment. Excited about seeing Misha, whom Brody hadn't seen since he had taken them home from the hospital.

That excitement was nowhere to be found right now, and she hated that Misha made him feel rejected. He could reject her all he wanted, but to reject Brody?

What was it he'd said at her first appointment? That he would never penalize someone for something they had no control over.

Well, from Lyndsey's perspective, he

was doing exactly that. Penalizing Brody for something he'd had no control over.

Sleeping with him had obviously been a mistake. At least for him. And if she'd known the consequences of giving in to her fantasies, she would have never let things head in that direction. She would have shown him to her spare bedroom and wished him a snippy good night.

But she'd had no idea Misha was capable of transforming into this cold stranger who had gotten what he wanted and then walked away without a second glance. It made her feel cheap. Something she hadn't felt since Wade. That had always been the difference between them. Misha had always made her feel special, while Wade made her feel like nothing.

"What are your goals for your other ear, Brody? The left one?"

Her son sat there in silence for a second, then he turned to look at her, and she could see from the expression on his face and the quivering of his lips that he was on the edge of breaking down. And she wasn't going to let that happen. Not in front of Misha.

She stood, pulling Brody up with her, and lifted her chin as she stared icy daggers at Misha. "This appointment is over. We've heard all we need to hear. When you can be bothered to set up a time for his next surgery, please give *me* a call."

With that she hustled Brody out of the office, right past the office assistant—who tried to call them back—and out into the hallway, where Brody immediately fell apart.

She held him in her arms, pulling him close and murmuring to him.

When he finally looked up, scrubbing at his face with his knuckles, he whispered. "Why does he suddenly hate me?"

Oh, God. She closed her eyes to keep from weeping for a boy who looked lost and confused. "He doesn't hate you."

He might hate her, but he didn't hate Brody. Her son was simply collateral damage for whatever was going on between Misha and her.

"Then why is he acting like that."

"Come with me. I want to tell you something." She wasn't going to tell him about what had transpired a week ago in their house. But she could tell him a little about her and Misha's past.

They made it to the cafeteria and Lyndsey got them each a drink and headed for a table in a far corner where people were less likely to hear what she had to say. They sat.

"You remember I told you that Misha and I went to school together?"

He nodded.

Pulling in a deep breath, she forced the next words from her mouth. "Well, it was a little more than that. We were close. Very close."

"You dated him?"

"Yes."

"That's wonderful, I think. Did you break up or something?"

She took a long pull of her drink as memories of their last day together trailed icy fingers over her. "Something like that. He had to move back to Belarus with his family."

"And you never saw him again?"

"Nope. Not until the first appointment I made with him."

Brody seemed to mull that over. "So he's decided he no longer wants to date you, is that what this is about?"

Leave it to her son to break things down into their most basic components. "I think that's exactly what this is about. He's taking a few steps backward and trying to return to a more professional relationship. It has nothing to do with you personally."

"But not dating you doesn't mean he can't be friends with me, right?"

"You would think that would be the case, but human relationships are more complicated than that."

Brody seemed to relax into his chair with a smile. "Well, in that case, thanks for ruining things for me, Mom."

That made her laugh. He could pin it on her all he wanted. She would welcome it, in fact. That did not mean Misha wasn't still in the hot seat. Oh, not by a long shot. It was just something she was not going to do in front of her son. "You're welcome." She gave him a mock bow from her seat.

"Hey, I'm going to ask Brittany to take you home, okay? This is about the time she gets off. I have a few things here at the hospital to take care of." She didn't tell him what or with whom.

He shrugged and then said, "Misha didn't say I couldn't listen to any music, right? I just can't listen to anything loud for the next few weeks."

"That seems to be what I remember, why?"

"We're going to try to nail down the melody to that new song we've been working on this afternoon. If that's okay with you, that is."

"It's fine. Just don't do anything you know you shouldn't do. That prosthesis has to last a very long time."

"Don't worry. I'll be careful."

She looked at him. "So your hearing is better. How much better."

He smiled, his eyes finally showing some sparkle again. "It's a lot better."

"That is exactly what I was hoping for."

They waited for Brittany out in front of the hospital. When she glanced at her watch, she saw it was almost noon. Misha normally took a two-hour lunch break if she remembered correctly.

Once Brittany arrived, she waved goodbye with a wide smile on her face. Her friend was taking Brody back to her place rather than dropping him off at home. Misha had kind of gotten her spooked about that, despite her calls to both the courthouse and her lawyer. But it was better to err on the side of caution, wasn't that how the saying went? Besides, she wouldn't be away from home for long. She just needed to have a word with a certain clueless ENT.

She went back into the hospital and headed for the elevator. Once on the floor where his office was, she went straight to the reception desk and smiled at the staff member. "Is Dr. Lukyanov finished with his morning patients? I'd like to have a word if so."

"Um…well, he normally goes to lunch now."

"That's okay, it won't take long. If you could just let him know that Lyndsey would like to speak with him for a moment. If he can't right now, I'll catch him on the floor tomorrow."

He couldn't run forever. They were eventually going to stand face-to-face. And she was pretty sure he'd rather do this in private than in front of the nurses on the floor, although she wasn't opposed to doing exactly that.

The woman picked up her phone, turning her back to Lyndsey and speaking in low tones. Lyndsey moved away from the desk so that she didn't appear to be eavesdropping on their conversation.

A minute later, the woman nodded at the door that led to the exam areas. "He'll see you in his office."

She sent her a brilliant smile. "Thanks so much."

Pushing through the double doors as if she had every right to be there, she turned the corner and then strolled down the hallway. She was going to arrive when she was good and ready. No rushing or nervous stuttering. She was going to say what she had to say and then leave.

She got to his office. The door was already open, so she went in. He looked up. "Lyndsey."

One corner of her mouth quirked up, even though nothing about this situation was funny. "You didn't tell me that sleeping with you carried a lifetime penalty for everyone associated with me."

"Excuse me?"

"You know exactly what I'm trying to say. You hurt my son in there with your little act. We left that room, and he bawled in my arms, thinking that you hate him."

Misha leaned back in his chair and closed his eyes. When they opened again, they were rife with an emotion she didn't understand. "I did what I had to do."

"You had to spit out orders and edicts to a fifteen-year-old boy without even asking him how his day was? What his band was working on?"

"I treated him the same way I would treat any patient."

She shook her head. "I don't believe that for a second."

"Believe what you like." He shot the

words at her like bullets, each one hitting their mark.

They stared at each other, and she wasn't exactly sure what else she could say or what she even hoped to accomplish here. Try to reason with his softer side?

Kind of hard when apparently that part of him had been sent into exile. If it had even been there in the first place. Had it all been an act?

He was the first one to break the charged silence. "Look, Lyndsey, if I don't pull back, I can no longer be his doctor. It's as simple as that. I'll have to refer him elsewhere."

"What?" Shock went through her. He was now threatening to not do Brody's next surgery? She'd been spitting mad, yes, but she hadn't said anything inappropriate, so she had no idea where any of this was coming from.

He blew out a breath and got up and shut the door, before coming to sit beside her. "There's a reason doctors can't operate on their relatives or loved ones. Their emotions can cloud their judgment, making it more dangerous for the patient."

He sounded like he was reading something straight from the hospital's personnel manual. "Did someone say something to you about me or Brody?"

"No. But I care about him. Maybe too much. I thought if I reeled myself in and changed my approach, I could go back to where I should be, which is looking at Brody as a patient rather than someone who means a lot to me."

"I trust you to do your job."

"Maybe *you* do. But in the end, that's not what matters. I have to trust myself enough to do my job. And I'm not sure I do right now."

"I see." Her mouth twisted as she tried to think. "So this was your idea of a solution? You don't think you could have talked to Brody and explained that to him. He's actually a pretty smart kid. He probably would have been fine with it. As it is, I'm not sure he'll agree to go through with the second surgery after today's visit."

"*Proklyatiye.* That was never my intention, Lyndsey. But I realized after being with you that I'd crossed a line I never should have crossed. Not while Brody was my patient."

"It wasn't like you seduced me. We were once involved. That has to count for something. Besides, I seem to remember being the one to climb into your lap, not the other way around."

Misha grinned. "Okay, that's an image I'm going to have a hard time erasing from my head." He touched her hand. "So what can I do to make things right with Brody?"

"Talk to him. Tell him you need to stay on professional footing with him until after the second surgery. He'll understand, I promise. And at least I won't have a confused and upset son who thinks he's done something wrong."

"Jesus, I never intended to send him that kind of message."

"Well, you did. I thought the same thing he did. Oh, not that he'd done something wrong, but that you regretted sleeping with me so much that you were going to brush us off every chance you got. And if it was that, I could handle it. But Brody can't. He's a sensitive kid—a musician who feels everything deeply. He doesn't understand adults who can turn their feelings on and off with the flick of a switch."

"And you think I can do that?"

"Apparently."

Misha turned to her and before she could say anything, he leaned over and kissed her mouth. Softly. Gently. "This is what I wanted to do the entire time you and Brody were in the room. Does that sound like someone who can turn their emotions… er…on and off at the flip of a switch?"

"You wanted to kiss me?"

"*Da*. And it's part of my problem. If something goes wrong in that operating room, will it be because my mind is somewhere else or something that would have happened whether or not you and I are involved?"

He thought there was a chance they could be involved? That was news to her. And there'd been no hint of any of that in the exam room.

"Are all Belarusians able to set aside their emotions at the drop of a hat?"

"When there is a need, I think. When it would hurt someone else if they don't."

She finally understood. "And you thought it would hurt Brody in the long run if you hadn't acted the way you had during his appointment."

"I think going to another surgeon would hurt him in the long run."

If his words were taken at face value, someone might think that Misha was conceited as hell. Well, he wasn't. She knew he had more experience with the procedure in this part of Louisiana than anyone else in his field. It was what had made Lyndsey come to him in the first place, telling him she didn't want to uproot Brody unless it was absolutely necessary. "I agree."

"I mean he could go to a surgeon in another state, like Texas, but that would be a lot of driving. And it's better to have whoever put in the first prosthesis fit the second one as well, so that there's as little variation as possible between the left and right ears."

She saw how that would be true.

"Then will you talk to him?" She hesitated. "I already told him that we were once involved with each other in high school."

"We were a little more than involved, don't you think?"

Her lips twisted. "I wasn't going to get into the nitty gritty facts of our relationship with my son. But I did say that it had maybe played a factor in how you acted toward him today."

His fingers dragged through his hair in that way that made her tummy shimmy inside of her. And discovering the reasons for his behavior had helped mitigate her anger quite a bit.

"And I don't have to say anything about that night at your house."

"No. I'd rather you didn't, in fact."

He tilted his head. "Then I'll talk to him. Where do you suggest?"

"Maybe somewhere neutral, off hospital grounds. Maybe at one of his jam sessions?" She hurried to say, "It doesn't mean you have to start going to all of his practices or start palling around with him. He'll understand, once you explain it to him. I know he will. But it has to come from you, rather than me."

"I understand. And after his second surgery?"

"What do you mean?"

"Is there any chance we can see each other periodically?"

Shock held her silent for a minute or two. "Y-you *want* to start seeing me?"

"It's a possibility. I'd want to take it slowly and see where it leads."

"I'm all for going slow."

He gave a smile that lit up his face. "That's not what I experienced recently."

Relief made her words flow a little more freely than maybe they should have, but she couldn't resist. "Oh, no? Well, I'm all for trying again. *After* Brody's second surgery, that is."

"In that case, we'll see where we are in a couple months' time."

A couple of months had never seemed so far away. But it was a smart plan. And a better alternative to trying to find another doctor. A surgeon she didn't know or trust. She wanted Misha on his case, and just like in the beginning of this journey, she was willing to do anything to make that happen. Even wait on her own happiness.

And did he make her happy?

Yes, she thought he did. And that was as far as she was willing to explore that thought. At least for the time being.

CHAPTER TEN

OVER THE NEXT couple of weeks, Misha found himself letting his guard down more and more while keeping to the boundaries they'd jointly set:

Rule number one: no sex.

That seemed obvious enough.

Rule number two: no sly touches or innuendos.

Rule number three: no kissing.

This one was personally hard for him, because he found himself wanting to do that every time he was in a room with her.

Rule number four: no waggling eyebrows.

When he'd made up that last rule, she challenged it by saying she never did that with her brows. He countered by saying yes, she did, and she knew it. Just like she'd done years ago. And they'd waggled a lot back then. Lyndsey had smacked him in the arm, which he'd claimed violated rule number two.

There'd been some laughter that had made him think it might just be possible to be friends during this interim time before Brody's second surgery, which was scheduled for two months from now. Surely they could hold out until then.

He moved across the nurses' area on his way to a patient's room. Lyndsey came up beside him and passed him a note. Then she turned and headed the other way.

When he looked down at the scrap of paper, the words *waggle-waggle* were scribbled across it. He laughed before crumpling the paper up and stuffing it in his scrubs.

Right then it hit him. He loved her. Had probably never stopped loving her. Maybe that's why there'd never been any real interest in dating other women, either when he was in Belarus or after he'd moved back to the States.

Did she feel the same about him?

He pulled the note out of his pocked and opened it up, smoothing it on one of the desks. *Waggle-waggle*. That would seem to indicate she might. Why else write something like that if she wasn't showing some kind of affection toward him?

Maybe she did. Maybe she wasn't yet sure. But that was a conversation to be had after Brody's next surgery. He was doing his damnedest to do right by the kid, so he wasn't going to ruin it all by skipping over the steps they'd laid out. They had all the time in the world, from what he was seeing. He just had to stay the course until he could come right out and say the words. But that time was not yet, and recently he'd read a journal article about a family who was suing their son's doctor for gross misconduct after their son died on the operating table. They claimed he was no longer able to be an objective party after the doctor fell in love with the boy's mother. Yes, it was different in that there was a love triangle involved, and in the fact that he couldn't see Lyndsey suing him for sleeping with her. But it still seemed wise to be careful. *Waggle-waggle* or no *waggle-waggle*.

The next day, Lyndsey spotted Misha walking across the lobby floor, just as she was coming from a patient's room. She wanted to ask him about another patient, so she rounded the corner to catch up with him.

She realized as she moved closer that he was on the phone with someone, and he was speaking in Russian. His words were crisp and succinct. No nonsense. In their time together as kids, she'd picked up some words here and there, and before she could move away, she heard the word Belarus and that whatever it was, Misha was going to think about it.

Something sharp struck her heart and went deep. Was he thinking of leaving again?

A sick sense of déjà vu came over her. Of course he would go back to visit his family—his mom. Just as she would if she'd been in his shoes. But what if this wasn't that? What if there was a business opportunity or the chance to head up the ENT department at a prestigious hospital over there? Misha would be quite a catch for a hospital in any part of the world.

She swallowed, knowing she was probably overreacting. But her dad had never really reentered her life once he'd left it. He'd withdrawn both emotionally and physically, always making promises he'd never kept. And she'd seen firsthand how Misha could withdraw emotionally when he wanted—or needed—to.

And hadn't Brody told her just yesterday that he wanted to learn Russian in case Misha needed to move back to Belarus? Had Misha hinted that he might?

She couldn't go through that again. Couldn't watch him fly away and wonder if he was going to end up being like her dad. Misha had been in the States for ten years now. Ten years and he never wondered about what happened to her. Whether she was alive or dead or living with a man who had almost killed her. If she'd known he was back in the States, would she have tried to call him?

Yes. She thought she would have.

But to live with that fear all over again, knowing he might walk away and not look back? That wasn't her. And she was pretty sure she couldn't be with someone who was capable of it. And she had Brody to think about. He'd understood Misha's reasons for being standoffish, but she was hoping after his surgery, they could go back to being friends.

But if Misha went back to Belarus and dropped off the face of the planet, her son would be crushed. And while she knew she'd never do anything stupid the next time around, like jump into bed with the first guy who looked her way, she was not sure how Brody would react. Would he turn moody and depressed like he'd been in the exam room that day when he'd thought Misha hated him? Or maybe something worse?

Maybe it was time to be proactive and ask him outright if he was thinking of moving back to his home country. And if he was? Well, then she was going to have to do one of the hardest things she'd ever done and tell him there could be no future for them if he was.

"Hey, can I talk to you for a minute?"

Misha looked up from the chart he was reading and smiled at her. "Sure, come on in."

She hesitated for a second or two before coming into the space and sitting down. Well…it wasn't actually sitting. It was more like she was perched, ready to take flight at any moment.

He frowned. "What's up?"

"The other day on the floor I was coming around the corner to say something to you and I realized you were on your phone with someone. Before I could turn around and leave you to your conversation, you mentioned Belarus and said you'd think about something."

His brows went up. "You understood all of that? I'm impressed."

"So I was right?"

"About what?"

She moistened her lips in a way that drew his attention, just like it always did. The woman was a distraction like none other had ever been. But that made sense, didn't it? He'd never been in love before. Not really.

"Are you thinking about going back to Belarus?"

He leaned back in his chair. "Is that what this is about? You thought I might be moving back there?"

"So you're not?"

"No, I'm not. There's a conference on otosclerosis that my mom thought I might be interested in presenting at. I told her I would think about it." The reason he hadn't said yes right away was precisely for this reason. He knew that Belarus was a touchy subject with her because of their past.

"I see."

There was something about the tone of her voice that gave him pause. "What do you see?"

"Can you think of a circumstance that might have you actually moving back there?"

What exactly was she trying to say? "Is there a reason why you're asking this?"

Her mouth twisted. "You haven't exactly answered my question."

He thought carefully about what to say. "I would never dare to predict the future. But there are a couple of reasons I might think about going back for an extended stay."

"As in months? Or years?"

"My answer would be, it depends. My dad died while I was in Belarus. If my mother became ill like he did, I would go back and care for her. It would be my duty as her son, in my culture. But it is also because she is my mother. Would you not do the same for Brody if the situation was reversed?"

"But it's not. Brody lives here in the States."

"And my mother prefers to live in Belarus. I will not uproot her from her home."

"I'm not asking you to. What I'm asking is…" She shook her head, her lower lip trembling as if she was trying to contain some terrible emotion. "God, Misha. I… I know you would need to go back. I would never expect you not to. But is there a time limit on any of that? You were gone for five years the last time you left. I'm just not sure I could go through that again."

"And yet I've been here in the States for ten. Longer than I was gone. Military families deal with this kind of absence all the time. Is it really so different?"

"In the life of a child, five years is forever. The milestones that would be missed, the growth that will happen. Could you really pull yourself away for that long?"

"We haven't even talked about children yet." His words were shorter than they should have been. He could chalk it up to impatience, but he wasn't sure that was all of it. This was like the past all over again. He couldn't make the promises she seemed to want him to make.

"Again, you've avoided the question rather than answering it. And I was talking about Brody. Not children of our own." Her voice wasn't as soft as it was a minute ago. Then she closed her eyes for a long minute. "I think I have to walk away, Misha. I know there are people who live apart for extended periods of time. Years even. But

I'm not wired that way. I can't do it. And realistically, you've said yourself there are times when you might have to leave for years. So I think it's better to pull the word relationship from our vocabulary and go back to being colleagues. Or friends even."

So she was allowed to move heaven and earth for her family, while he was not afforded the same luxury? He didn't think so.

"If you think we could ever be friends with the conditions you've put on our relationship, you are very much mistaken. If it ends here, it ends here for good. We may have to work together. But one thing we don't have to be is friends."

Her lower lip trembled again for a second before it returned to normal. "And Brody?"

"What about him?"

"Please don't hurt him. We don't have to be friends, but please don't punish him for my inability to deal with the realities of being in a relationship with you."

He saw her point. "In that, you won't have to worry. Brody will always be special to me. And I'll make sure I don't make him feel any less than the great kid he is."

"Thank you."

His brows went up. "How do you say it here in Louisiana? It's been real. See you around."

She didn't say anything else, she simply got up from her chair, turned and walked out of his office and out of his life. And he couldn't think of anything that would change the outcome. He couldn't promise he would never go back for an extended period of time. And she couldn't deal with the possibility that he might. So he didn't try to stop her. Didn't try to feed her lies and make promises that he might not be able to keep down the road. To do that would be no better than what her ex-husband had done when he promised to change his ways. So he did what the old adage said: when you loved someone, you set them free.

Two weeks after her conversation with Misha, Lyndsey did two things. She found out that Wade had moved away from his hometown, which was a huge relief, and she decided that she was making a job move back to Centerville for good. She'd given her notice at Louisiana Southern. The other nurses had tried to talk her out of it but had finally accepted her excuse that after a year of trying, the hour-long commute had simply become too much. They'd given her a small going-away party, one that Misha hadn't attended. Not that she'd expected him to. She'd contacted him only once to make sure that he was still willing to do Brody's surgery that had been moved up to just a few short weeks away. His answer had been curt and to the point. He'd said he would do it, and she'd find he didn't go back on his promises.

She found herself not going to as many of Brody's garage practices after seeing Misha's Jeep pull up once. She'd made a beeline out of there so she wouldn't have to say anything to him. Even seeing him made a fire ignite in the acid that now hung out in her stomach on a regular basis. But one thing she was glad of was that he was maintaining his relationship with her son. There was always a risk of seeing him, but it was a risk she was willing to take.

Not like the risk of having someone she loved leave the country for good.

Wait. Back up a minute. She loved him?

Of course she did. Why else would she write him off the way she had?

Except she'd just now realized it. She loved him. Was terrified of being hurt by him again like she had been in the past. Like her father had hurt her. But Misha, in leaving the last time, had never sealed off wanting to keep in contact. Of wanting to try to have a long-distance relationship. She was the one who'd done that.

He'd been willing to live with the risk of it not working out. Of being gutted if she walked away. And she *had* been the one to walk away. Misha might have left the country, but *she'd* been the one to leave the relationship.

She hadn't been able to go with him back then. She'd still been in her late teens living with her parents. But now she was an adult, with the adult ability to make choices she hadn't been able to make back then.

And weren't there risks to everything in life? There'd been the risk of Brody going deaf. Had she cast him aside because of it? No. She'd learned sign language and prepared for the possibility. Why couldn't she do the same for Misha? Why couldn't she prepare for the possibility and find a way to make it work? Just like she'd done with her son. Because she loved him. Loved them both.

But how? How could she prepare for another five-year absence? Like Misha said, military families did it. Some of them lived overseas with their deployed loved ones, when possible. Some settled for daily video chats. They made it work. Because they loved each other. Lyndsey could see that she'd been totally selfish. It was no wonder he said they could never be friends. Because she hadn't acted like one. At least not like a good one. It had been her way or the highway, and she could see how wrong she'd been, both now and fifteen years ago. They could have found a way to make it work, but she'd chosen not to. And now she realized she'd handled both situations like a child.

So she had a choice. She could go on act-

ing like a child, or she could do some grow-
ing up and figure out a way to make things
with Misha work. If he was even willing to
after everything she'd said to him.

Her lips twisted. Maybe that was part
of what being an adult meant—going to
someone and trying to make amends. Apol-
ogizing and then acting on that apology,
making changes that would prove you really were sorry. And then, after all that, if
Misha no longer wanted to maintain a relationship or even friendship, then it was
something she would have to accept. Because it was the grown-up thing to do.

But she'd already quit her job in Lafayette. Well…an hour wasn't so far away in
the scheme of things, was it? But first she
had to find out if Misha even wanted to
make it work.

And she prayed for both her sake and
Brody's that saying she was sorry wasn't
too little too late.

"Misha, I have someone out front who
would like to have a word with you, if you
have a minute."

Great. He was bone tired and had been

looking forward to going home and eating some cold cornflakes and milk for dinner. Then he could mope until it was time to go to bed. He had a feeling he'd be doing a lot of that over the coming months.

"Is it a patient, Marie?"

"Not exactly, but she is related to a patient."

His heart jolted for a second before he remembered that a lot of his patients were kids and were brought in by their parents or other relatives. It didn't mean it was Lyndsey. He hadn't heard from her since that terse phone call three weeks ago. He'd actually gone to a couple of Brody's garage practices and only realized afterward that part of the reason he went was the hope that he might catch sight of her. His declaration that they couldn't be friends had been a ridiculous attempt to force her hand. But he hadn't been all wrong. She couldn't expect him to never visit his home country any more than he could expect her to never visit Brody should he move away someday.

"Misha?"

Marie was waiting for an answer. He

shoved his hand into his pocket and felt
something crinkle as he did. A piece of
paper. He pulled it out and saw something
familiar scribbled there. He turned it side-
ways to read it. *Waggle-waggle*.

Hellfire. That seemed like years ago,
when in reality it had only been a few short
weeks.

There had to be a way to get back to that.
Or at least try.

He finally said, "Tell them I'll meet them
out in reception."

And then once he was done with that, he
was going to make a very difficult phone
call. But it had to be done if he expected
to have any kind of closure.

He set the note on his desk, smoothing
it out. When he got back, it would serve
as a reminder of why he was going to do
what he hadn't done fifteen years ago and
call her, even if she said she didn't want to
hear from him. And since she'd quit her
job at Louisiana Southern, she'd made it
pretty plain that she'd cut ties with him and
had no plans to see him again, except for
Brody's next surgery. Well, she was going

to hear from him one last time, whether she wanted to or not. And then he would know for sure if it was truly over or if it was something that could be revived with enough time and effort, both of which he was willing to put in, if she was willing to do the same. With that decision made, he walked out to reception.

And came face-to-face with the very woman he'd been thinking of.

"What are you doing here?"

"Sorry for coming unannounced. It seems like I make a habit of doing that."

"I'm sorry?" He had no idea what she was talking about. Had she come by when he wasn't here?

"You didn't know who I was at our first meeting, and that was my doing."

"Ah yes. I think I was just as shocked to see you then as I am now."

She paused, glancing at where Marie was still working on some patient files on her monitor. "Is there someplace we can talk?"

"Come back to my office." He was trying very hard to believe this was something about Brody and not about them, because if he let hope creep in where it wasn't wanted, he would be gutted when all she wanted to talk about was a scheduling need.

The last time she'd been back here, she'd broken things off with him. Maybe he should have chosen someplace like the courtyard, where those specters weren't lurking, waiting to say "I told you so" when he was wrong about the possibility of finding a compromise.

He closed the door and motioned her to a chair. But this time, instead of sitting behind his desk, he came around to sit next to her.

Before he could say anything, she started talking. "You know, I thought I had learned all about taking risks when Brody got his diagnosis. I hoped for the best, but planned for the worst. I fought with all I had to get him the help he needed. But on the side, I was busy learning sign language. Just in case. And neither Brody nor I had known the other was studying it until the surgery, when he signed to me. And I signed back."

Misha blinked. "I didn't know that."

"No one did." She smiled. "So yeah, I thought I knew all about risk. Thought I was pretty much an expert on it. Until I overheard a small part of your phone conversation with your mom and almost made the same mistake that I made fifteen years ago. I realized I knew nothing about real risk. The kind that forces you to make sacrifices—big ones—because you love that person."

The tentacles of hope that he'd been trying to keep from gaining a foothold ripped down a whole wall and sauntered in. He made no move to stop it. Because she'd said three very important words. Risk, sacrifice, and love.

Because he realized when he'd been thinking about calling her, those three words had not been very far from his mind, either.

He smiled. "That's funny. You know what I realized just a few minutes ago?"

She shook her head.

"I realized that this..." he reached across the desk and pulled that slip of paper toward him and held it up. "These words scribbled on a piece of paper make the risks seem a little less scary, they make the sacrifices seem a little bit smaller, and they make the love worth fighting for."

"You kept that?"

"Not on purpose. But it seems that it was kept there *for* a purpose, maybe by some higher power, so I could find it again at the right moment." He took a deep breath and said the words. "I love you, Lynds. And as long as you waggle your brows at me, everything in my life will have meaning and purpose and fulfillment. No matter the risks. No matter the sacrifices."

She stared at him before reaching over and touching his face as if in wonder. "I realized almost the exact same thing. Not about the waggly brows—I still deny doing that—but that love makes all the rest worthwhile."

He hesitated before asking. "And if I ever have to go to Belarus for an extended stay?" He held his breath as he waited for her answer.

"Well, then you'd better start teaching

me some Russian so I don't look like a total goofball to your family and friends."

He laughed. "You could never look like a goofball—whatever that is." His smile faded. "And what about Brody? You think he'd be okay coming with us, if he's still a minor?"

"Here's the funny thing about Brody. He's already been preparing, even before he knew I was coming here. He secretly bought a well-known study program and has been studying Russian. Because, in his words, 'If he ever moves back to Belarus, I'm going to go visit him.' How's that for being a risk-taker?"

"I truly love that kid." A thought just occurred to him. "But—"

"If this is about his surgery, listen. This is a risk both Brody and I are willing to take. If you choose not to do his surgery and want another surgeon to take over, we'll be okay with that decision. We'll just find the next best surgeon and worm our way into their heart the same way we did yours."

He laughed. God. It felt so good to be

able to feel true joy again. "Just don't worm too hard, because the only one who is allowed to love you with the love of a family is me. Well, and your blood relatives, of course." He stopped for a minute before saying. "You'll really be okay if I feel too attached to do the surgery? I'm not even sure the hospital will let me, unless we hide our relationship. Which I'm not willing to do."

"So are you saying we have a relationship?"

"Oh, yes, we have a relationship."

She leaned over and kissed him, and the touch was sweeter than anything they'd done before. Because this touch had a promise none of the others had had. The promise of forever, and that was something he never wanted to take for granted ever again.

"Except this time no rules. I want to be able to waggle my eyebrows whenever I choose to, no matter who is around. I just have to learn how to do it first."

"Agreed." A subject came to mind that he wanted to clear up, because he'd thrown something at her in anger the last time they were together. "About children…"

Her face clouded. "If you don't want any, that's okay. It's a sacrifice I'm willing to make."

"Oh, but I do want them, and given our ages…"

"Excuse me?"

"I'm not calling you old. All I'm saying is we might want to start trying sooner rather than later. I don't think I'll have the energy to have kids when I'm ninety."

"Hmm. I bet you'll be a pretty sexy ninety-year-old."

"Are you calling me pretty? Or pretty sexy?"

"Once your receptionist finishes with those files, I think we should lock this door and find out. Although to be honest, I do find you pretty, in the most masculine sense. And those eyes…they just do it for me."

Misha picked up his cell phone and dialed Marie's extension. She picked up almost immediately. "I just wanted to see how you're coming with those files. I don't want you to have to work too late." He glanced at Lynds. "So you've just finished the last one? Great. Have a wonderful evening, and I'll see you in the morning." With that, he pressed the button to end the call. "She's done."

"So I heard. So all that's left is for you to get up and lock that door."

The last thing he saw as he went to do just that was Lyndsey trying to waggle her brows at him. It didn't look quite as sexy as he'd envisioned. But it was still adorable.

He stifled a laugh. This could prove to be quite interesting. But one thing he knew for sure was that this room was going to be filled with love. And promises that would be kept no matter the risk. No matter the sacrifice. Because love was worth it all.

EPILOGUE

THEY WERE GETTING MARRIED.

In Belarus.

She could hardly believe it was really happening. But it was.

She and Brody had arrived two weeks ago, and Misha had met them at the airport. She'd wanted it that way, wanted him to be able to go and arrange things with his family and friends. His mom had been lovely and understanding and had welcomed her and Brody into the family with open arms.

Biting her lip, she waited at the back of the huge cathedral and looked in wonder at the beauty all around her. A hand squeezed hers, and she turned to look at Brody who was smiling at her. "Imagine the acoustics in this place."

She laughed, then covered her mouth

when it echoed through the space. "Do not make me laugh."

"You've been laughing a lot recently. I like the sound of it. Actually, I like the sound of everything. I'll never take my hearing for granted again."

Her son had had the surgery on his other ear. And it had been performed by Misha's mentor, the one who'd overseen his training in the technique. They'd had to go all the way to New York to have it done, but it had been worth it.

The strains of an organ sounded at the front of the space. "I think it's time."

"Are you sure you want me to walk you down the aisle, Mom?"

She hugged him close. "More sure than anything."

"It's kind of like the baby is walking you down the aisle too, isn't it?"

"Shh…"

"Oh, right. Sorry."

She and Misha had found out a month ago that they were expecting a child, which was why he'd made the trip to Belarus to fast-track their wedding. No one knew about the pregnancy yet, except their little family, and she wanted to keep it that way for right now. Just for a little while longer. Once they got back to the States, they would have a second smaller wedding with her mom and their friends in attendance. And the funny thing was, it didn't feel like a sacrifice to either of them.

She and Brody started their trek down the long, carpeted aisle, her eyes locking with Misha's as he stood tall and proud at the front of the cathedral.

It seemed to take forever to reach him, but reach him she did. And when he took her hand to escort her up the steps, a shiver went through her. Just like it did every time he touched her. She suspected it would always be this way. They may have gotten off to a late start, but they both intended to finish this race well. And to finish it together.

A clergyman recited words she barely understood, but Misha had gone over what she needed to say and when. And he nodded at her, whispering a word to her when she stumbled over the pronunciation, but she was proud and happy to stand beside him. To finally be able to declare to the world that they belonged together.

When it was time for him to kiss her, they clung together for a little longer than was customary, judging by the titter of laughter that came from behind them. They broke apart and turned to face the relatives who'd gathered there to celebrate with them. Her eyes sought out Brody, surprised when she saw he had a microphone in his hand.

"What?" she whispered to Misha, only to have him say, "He and I both agreed this was the perfect way to celebrate the start of our new family."

From somewhere behind her came the familiar notes that she'd heard time and time again in a garage in Centerville, Louisiana. Her glance swung to Misha with an unspoken question.

"Yes, they're all here, actually." He nodded to a place she hadn't noticed when she came down the aisle. But Brody's band members were all there, playing a song she knew by heart. And he was right. The acoustics were out of this world. She had no idea how any of them had managed this, but she was beyond grateful.

Then her son's voice came to her, singing words that were filled with a wistfulness and a question that only the listeners could answer.

As I sit here in my silence, wondering what is next,
The fear is overwhelming.
Is there really nothing left?
Then a tiny blip of sound bursts through my brokenness.
Just a hint of treble. Followed by a touch of bass.
Is any of this possible?
Can a miracle break through?
Or is it all a wishful dream that never will come true.

As tears poured down her face, she knew it wasn't just a dream. It was reality. Their reality. And it only promised to get better with time.

She squeezed Misha's hand and looked up at him, trying to contain the huge ball of emotion that grew and grew with every breath she took. Looking up at the man she loved as the song drew to a close, she did the only thing she could think of. Sent a message that only the man she loved could fully comprehend: she waggled her brows at him.

* * * * *

*If you enjoyed this story, check out
these other great reads from
Tina Beckett*

The Nurse's One-Night Baby
The Vet, the Pup and the Paramedic
A Family Made in Paradise
From Wedding Guest to Bride?

All available now!